TOXIC

STALKER VS. STALKER

MILLY TAIDEN

ABOUT THE BOOK

I never wanted to be obsessed with anyone.

But Hawk Rivers isn't just anyone.

He's the devil in a tailored suit, a man who can bring empires to their knees with a single phone call.

He's willing to kill without remorse for what he considers his.

And he's decided that I belong to him.

What he doesn't know is, he's already mine.

If his obsession runs deep, mine is *toxic*.

They say you should be careful what you wish for.

They never said anything about falling in love with it.

This isn't your typical love story.

It's a twisted dance of dominance that threatens to consume us both.

TOXIC

NEW YORK TIMES *and* USA TODAY
BESTSELLING AUTHOR
MILLY TAIDEN

This book is a work of fiction. The names, characters, places, and incidents are fictitious or have been used fictitiously, and are not to be construed as real in any way. Any resemblance to persons, living or dead, actual events, locales, or organizations is entirely coincidental.

Published By
Latin Goddess Press
Winter Springs, FL 32708
http://millytaiden.com
Toxic
Copyright © 2024 by Milly Taiden
Cover: Jacqueline Sweet
All Rights Are Reserved. No part of this book may be used or reproduced in any manner whatsoever without written permission, except in the case of brief quotations embodied in critical articles and reviews.
Property of Milly Taiden
September 2024

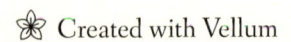

❈ Created with Vellum

For

—Jill

You encouraged me to write this on our trip to Australia and I finally did it. I had so much fun with it.

For

-Nevaeh
Thank you for pushing me to try something different.

In love and war...anything goes

ONE

DEVIN'S 18TH BIRTHDAY

The hotel ballroom is a kaleidoscope of masks and shimmering gowns, a dizzying display of wealth and excess. But I barely register any of it. My entire being is focused on her—Devin West.

It's her 18th birthday, and this lavish masquerade ball is supposedly in her honor, but she's tucked away in a shadowy corner as if trying to disappear into the ornate wallpaper.

The soft amber lights catch on her emerald mask, highlighting those striking green eyes that seem to take in everything and nothing at once. Her gown, a deep forest green that makes her pale skin glow, clings to curves I'm finding impossible to ignore. Dark hair cascades down her back in loose waves, and I'm seized by the urge to run my fingers through it.

I adjust my own mask, a sleek black design that matches my tailored suit. This is my first major event since taking over the family business, and the Rivers-West connection is too important to ignore. But business, for once, is the furthest thing from my mind.

Devin shifts slightly, and I'm mesmerized by the graceful movement. She leans in to whisper something to my sister Olivia, her best friend. It's the most animation I've seen from her all night, and I find myself straining to catch even a whisper of her voice.

"Hawk," my uncle John and his son Thomas stop beside me. "Didn't think you'd make it."

I glance at them before going back to watching Devin and Olivia. "Why not?"

"This isn't usually your scene, cousin," Thomas says. There's a slight sneer in his tone.

I glance at them again. "You don't know me enough to know my *scene*," I say, my voice dead cold.

My uncle clears his throat. "Yeah, well, when you have time, I'd like to talk to you about a project I think could be beneficial-"

I don't bother looking at them. "I'm not interested."

"You don't even know-" Thomas tries to intervene.

I glance at them again. "I said," I state with steel in my voice, "I'm not interested."

I dismiss them and go back to watching Devin.

"Mr. Rivers," a voice intrudes, and I tear my gaze away to find some faceless guest trying to engage me in conversation. I give him curt responses, my attention constantly drawn back to Devin like a magnet to true north.

She stands suddenly, excusing herself from Olivia. As she slips out of the ballroom, I make my decision in an instant.

"Excuse me," I mutter to the man still talking at me, not caring if it's rude. I follow Devin's path, keeping a discreet distance. The scent of her perfume—something floral with an underlying musk—lingers in the air, guiding me.

The hotel hallway outside is quieter, the sounds of the party muffled by thick carpet and heavy doors. I'm about to call out to her when I hear voices around the corner—sharp, cruel voices that make me pause.

"Well, well, well. Look who it is," a girl's voice sneers. I recognize it immediately as Regina Black, Devin's cousin and notorious mean girl. "The birthday girl herself, sneaking away from her own party. What's wrong, freak? Can't handle a little attention?"

I peer around the corner, and the scene before me makes my blood boil. Regina and two other girls—I vaguely recognize them as Brittany and Tasha—have Devin cornered. Their masks are pushed up, revealing faces twisted with malice.

"I—I just needed some air," Devin says softly, her eyes downcast. The tremor in her voice ignites a protective fury in me.

Regina laughs, the sound grating and cruel. "Air? Please. You're pathetic. Mommy and Daddy spent all this money on your stupid birthday, and for what? You're still the same awkward little nobody."

"God, it's embarrassing just looking at you," Brittany chimes in, her voice dripping with disdain. "Did you really think a fancy dress would make people actually like you?"

Tasha nods, a vicious smile on her face. "As if. You know what everyone's saying in there? That it's a waste. That you don't deserve any of this."

"Face it, Devin," Regina says, stepping closer. "You're nothing but a disappointment. To your family, to everyone. Why don't you do us all a favor and just disappear?"

She shoves Devin, hard. Devin stumbles back, her back hitting the wall with a soft thud. And something in me snaps.

Before I know it, I'm striding forward, my voice a low, dangerous growl. "Get away from her. Now!"

The girls whirl around, their eyes widening as they recognize me. Regina pales visibly but quickly tries to compose herself. "Hawk!" she exclaims, her voice suddenly syrupy sweet. "We were just having a little chat with our dear cousin. Girl talk, you know how it is."

"Do I know you well enough to be on a first name basis?" I snap.

"But, Mr. Rivers," she tries again.

"Save it," I snarl, cutting her off. I tower over them, using every inch of my height to intimidate. "Don't fuck with me, Regina. I'm not stupid. I heard everything."

Regina's fake smile falters. "Oh, come now, Mr. Rivers. We were just teasing. Devin knows we don't mean anything by it, don't you, Devin?"

I step closer, my voice dropping to a menacing whisper. "If I ever catch you or your little minions bothering her again, I will personally ensure that your lives become very, very unpleasant. Your family's standing, your social status, your future prospects—I can crush them all with a single phone call. Do I make myself clear?"

They nod frantically, mumbling apologies as they scurry away. I turn to Devin, my anger melting into concern as I see her trembling. She's pressed against the wall, her chest rising and falling rapidly with shallow breaths.

"Are you all right?" I ask, my voice softer now. I resist the urge to pull her into my arms, not wanting to overwhelm her.

She looks up at me, and for the first time, I hear her speak directly to me. "I'm fine," she says, her voice quiet but steadier than I expected. "Thank you, Mr. Rivers."

The sound of her voice catches me off guard. It's soft, yes, but there's a calm strength underneath I wasn't expecting. I find myself wanting to hear more of it, to uncover all the layers of Devin West.

"Hawk," I correct her gently. "Please, call me Hawk."

A small smile tugs at her lips, and my heart rate picks up. "Hawk," she repeats, and I decide then and there that I love the way my name sounds on her lips.

I notice her wobble slightly, the adrenaline likely wearing off, and make a quick decision. "Come on," I say, bending down to scoop her into my arms. "Let's get you somewhere quiet."

She lets out a small gasp of surprise but doesn't protest as I carry her to the elevator.

"I...I'm using the penthouse suite for the night," she says, her voice low.

I'm acutely aware of her warmth against my chest, the way she fits perfectly in my arms. Her head rests against my shoulder, and I feel her breath, warm and quick, against my neck.

In the penthouse suite, I gently set her on a plush sofa. "You shouldn't let them treat you like that," I say, taking a seat beside her. "You're worth so much more than their petty insults."

Devin looks down, fidgeting with the edge of her mask. "It's not that simple," she murmurs. "Regina, she... she knows how to hurt people. How to make you believe the worst about yourself."

"Look at me," I say, my tone gentle but firm. When she raises her eyes to meet mine, I'm struck by the depth of emotion I see there. And something else—a flicker of interest quickly hidden but not before I catch it.

I watch as her gaze drops to my lips for a fraction of a second before darting away. The attraction crackles between us, electric and undeniable. I lean in slightly, testing the waters, and I'm rewarded with a sharp intake of breath from Devin.

"You're beautiful," I say, my voice low and husky. "And strong. Believe me. Don't let anyone tell you otherwise."

A blush creeps up her cheeks, visible even beneath her mask. "I'm not—I mean, you're—" she stammers, and I find her nervousness endearing.

I reach out slowly, giving her time to pull away if she wants. When she doesn't, I gently remove her mask, then my own. Our eyes lock, and in that moment, I know with absolute certainty that she's it for me. There will never be anyone else.

I drink in every detail of her face—the delicate arch of her eyebrows, the smattering of freckles across her nose, the full curve of her lower lip. Her eyes, free from the mask, are even more captivating up close—a swirling mix of emerald and jade that I could lose myself in.

"Devin," I breathe, cupping her face in my hand. She leans into my touch, her eyes fluttering closed for a moment. The trust in that simple gesture makes my heart clench.

When she opens them again, the look she gives me is shy but unmistakably wanting. It awakens something primal in me, a need to protect her, to possess her. I want to wrap her in my arms and never let go, to shield her from the cruelties of the world while showing her pleasures she's never imagined.

But I resist, knowing she's not ready for all that yet. Instead, I lean in slowly, giving her plenty of time to stop me. When my lips finally meet hers, it's soft, chaste—a promise of things to come.

The kiss lasts only a moment, but it feels like a lifetime. Her lips are soft, yielding, and I have to summon every ounce of self-control not to deepen it, not to claim her mouth fully.

I pull back, watching her reaction carefully. Her eyes are wide, lips slightly parted in wonder. "Hawk," she whispers, and the way she says my name sends a shiver down my spine.

TWO

His lips leave mine, and the world stops spinning.

I open my eyes, not realizing I'd closed them. Hawk is watching me, his gaze intense, searching. I've seen him before at family events, always from afar. Always watching, never participating. Just like me. But now, here in this opulent suite away from prying eyes, he's close enough to touch. Close enough to taste.

My first kiss. With Hawk Rivers. The Devil. That's what everyone in my family calls him. He's mentally unstable they say. Cold. Calculating. Willing to kill his own family without batting an eye. He's perfect.

"Hawk," I whisper, his name a prayer on my lips.

Something flashes in his eyes—desire, possession,

something darker I can't quite name. It should frighten me. Instead, it ignites a fire low in my belly.

"So beautiful."

His words wash over me, soothing the raw edges left by Regina's cruelty. For years, I've endured her taunts and bullying. I've hidden in shadows, made myself small. But now, with Hawk looking at me like I'm the only person in the world, I feel something shift inside me.

I'm leaving for college in a few days. This might be my only chance. For once in my life, I'm going to take what I want.

Before I can second-guess myself, I surge forward, capturing Hawk's lips with mine. The kiss is clumsy, inexperienced, but fueled with pent-up longing. Hawk freezes for a moment, clearly caught off guard.

Then, gently but firmly, he pushes me back. "Devin, stop," he says, his voice strained. "You're not ready for this. For me."

Hurt and embarrassment flood through me. Of course. Someone like him would never want someone like me. Stupid, awkward Devin. Always misreading situations. I know I'm not right for him. Strong, commanding, and powerful Hawk. I'm just a socially awkward heiress who can't even get her cousins to respect her.

Yeah, my family comes to my rescue all the time, but I'm tired of it. I don't want to be that weak person anymore. Why would Hawk want a weakling like me? Why would he bother with me when I can barely stand up for myself?

"I'm sorry," I stammer, heat rushing to my cheeks. "I thought... I mean, you kissed me, so I assumed... God, I'm such an idiot."

I start to pull away, wanting nothing more than to flee and hide away and never show my face again. But Hawk's hand on my arm stops me.

"Devin, look at me," he commands, his tone brooking no argument.

Reluctantly, I meet his gaze. What I see there steals my breath. Gone is the careful control he's maintained all night. In its place is a raw, primal hunger that makes my pulse race.

His hand wraps around my throat and squeezes. He's holding the air in my lungs hostage. I don't care. If I die at this moment from his hands, I wouldn't regret a single second. The hand around my throat harshly pulls me close while his other hand slides into my hair and grips, turning my face up to his. I struggle to suck in a breath. My eyes water but I'm not afraid. I blink away the tears gathering in my eyes.

"It's not that I don't want you," he says, each word

deliberate and heavy with meaning. He slides his tongue over my bottom lip. "It's that once we start, I don't know if I'll be able to stop. And you deserve better than a rough fuck in a hotel suite."

His crude language shocks me, but it also sends a thrill through my body. I've never been spoken to like this before. Never been looked at with such naked want. He releases my throat and I feel slightly sad.

"I don't care," I hear myself say, surprising us both with my boldness. "I want you."

For a long moment, Hawk stares at me. I can see the battle raging behind his eyes—desire warring with restraint. Then, like a dam breaking, the careful control he's maintained all night snaps.

In an instant, he's on me. His kiss is rough, demanding, nothing like the gentle peck from before. His hands tangle in my hair, gripping to the point of pain. I should be scared. I should want to run.

Instead, I feel alive for the first time in my life.

I match his intensity, pouring every ounce of my frustration and longing into the kiss. When we finally break apart, we're both panting.

"Devin," he growls, and the sound sends shivers down my spine. "Last chance to back out. Are you absolutely sure about this?"

I meet his gaze, seeing the storm of desire and something darker swirling in his eyes. In this moment, I know there's no going back. Hawk Rivers has awakened something in me that can never be put to sleep again.

"I'm sure," I whisper and seal my fate with another kiss.

He takes several steps away from me and then pins me with his gaze.

"Take off your clothes, Devin," he commands, his voice leaving no room for argument. Not that I planned to.

I hesitate for a moment, but the intensity in his gaze has me complying. I strip down, my dress and underwear pooling at my feet, leaving me bare and vulnerable under his scrutiny. For a second, his gaze stops on my hip and stares. It's a tattoo I got myself for my birthday. A black snake curled around a moth.

He nods appreciatively, his eyes darkening with desire as he stalks around me. "You're fucking perfect," he murmurs, his voice thick with lust. "You're a damn wet dream, Devin."

I've spent so long feeling invisible, unwanted. But here, now, under Hawk's burning gaze, I feel like the most desirable woman in the world.

I blush, my body heating with embarrassment and

arousal. Seemingly satisfied, he sits in a chair several steps across from me, his legs spread wide, and beckons me forward with a crook of his finger.

"Crawl to me, sweetheart," he orders, a wicked smirk playing on his lips.

I drop to my hands and knees, the cool temperature sending shivers up my arms. I crawl to him, my eyes locked onto his, and I'm shocked to find that I love it. I love the way he's looking at me like he wants to devour me whole. I love the way my body responds to his commands.

I reach him, my hands resting on his knees, and he leans down, his lips brushing against my ear. "Undress me, Devin," he growls, sending another shockwave of desire through me.

My hands tremble as I unbutton his shirt, exposing his muscular chest. Wow. He looks even better than I could have imagined. His massive arms make my throat dry.

Next, I unbuckle his belt, my fingers fumbling with the zipper of his pants. He lifts his hips, allowing me to pull them down along with his boxers, freeing his cock.

It's hard and thick, standing at attention. This is my first time seeing a man naked, in person. I should be embarrassed but I'm too caught up in the moment. He's beautiful. All strength. My body aches with desire. I want him inside me, filling me, claiming me. I want him to make me his. I've never felt these emotions for anyone else. Ever.

Hawk Rivers is my birthday present, and I can't wait to unwrap him.

Hawk's hands grip my waist, and with an effortless show of strength, he lifts me onto his lap like I weigh nothing. I gasp as he settles me on top of him, my pussy grinding down on his hardness.

A low moan escapes his lips, the sound sending a shiver down my spine. "Fuck, Devin," he growls, his hands tightening on my hips. "I can't wait to stretch you out. To make you mine."

His words are filthy, wrong, but they turn me on even more. I roll my hips, coating his cock with my wetness, my breath hitching as the head of his cock brushes against my clit.

He leans in, his lips brushing against my neck and he sucks on my throat. I moan his name. He bites hard and then sucks again. I dig my nails into his shoulders, wanting to keep him close. Another bite and suck. My body is on fire. He continues to lick, suck and bite my throat and shoulders, leaving his mark as he goes. "Has anyone else had you, Devin?" he murmurs, his voice dark and possessive.

I shake my head, a moan escaping my lips as I continue to grind against him. "No," I gasp.

He pulls back, his gray eyes locking onto mine, intense and demanding. "Keep it that way," he orders, his voice leaving no room for argument. "I'm the only one who will touch you."

Before I can respond, he grips my hip with one hand, using the other to guide his cock to my entrance. He rubs the head against my wetness coating himself in my desire before slowly sinking me onto his cock.

I cry out as he fills me, stretching me wide. He's so big, and for a moment, I can't breathe. He pinches one of my nipples, rolling it between his fingers, sending a jolt of pleasure straight to my core.

"That's it, sweetheart," he murmurs, his voice thick with lust. "Take it all. Take every inch."

He helps me roll my hips, his hands guiding me as I slowly adjust to his size. The whole time he grunts out words that make me even wetter. "You're so fucking tight, Devin," he groans. "So fucking wet. You love this, don't you? You love having me buried deep inside you."

I nod, my breath coming in short gasps as I continue to ride him. He's stretching me, filling me, and it feels so fucking good. I can feel every inch of him, every ridge and vein as he slides in and out of me.

He leans in, his lips brushing against my ear. "You're mine now, Devin," he growls.

Once I'm stretched around him, his hips move with a force that leaves me breathless. "You're so good, Devin," he moans. "Riding me like you were made for it. You're going to come for me, aren't you? You're going to come all over my cock."

His words push me over the edge, and I cry out, my body convulsing as I come hard around him. One of his hands grips my throat tightly while the other squeezes my ass cheek to the point of pain. Then he smacks my ass, the sharp sting sending another wave of pleasure through me. "That's it, sweetheart," he groans, the hand around my throat squeezing. "Come for me. Make a mess all over my cock."

He swells inside me, growing even harder. He leans in, his lips brushing against mine, his breath hot on my face. "I'm going to fill you up, Devin," he growls. "You're mine now. Mine."

With a final thrust, he buries himself deep inside me, his cock pulsing as he comes. The hand around my throat squeezes at the same time his other hand grips my hair painfully and brings my face into his for a hard kiss. He comes inside me, filling me, marking me, claiming me. I collapse against him, my body spent, my breath coming in ragged gasps. He wraps his arms around me, holding me tightly, his cock still buried deep inside me.

"Happy birthday, Devin," he murmurs, his voice low and gravelly.

Hawk Rivers has claimed me, and even if it's just for today, I am his.

THREE

SIX YEARS LATER

The ballroom of the West family's flagship hotel pulses with opulence and power, a gilded cage for the city's elite. Crystal chandeliers cascade from the vaulted ceiling, their light fracturing into a thousand glittering points across the sea of designer gowns and tailored suits.

The air is thick with the heady scent of wealth—expensive perfumes, aged whiskey, and the intangible musk of ambition. Even after so many years of learning how to be a strong woman, this scene makes me uncomfortable.

People. They're not my thing. It's funny how I am so at home with my Hacker Alliance connections and employees more than I am with family. My own parents don't know who I am. They just know I'm gifted. A genius when it comes to computers, software, numbers and pretty much anything technical.

My genius made my childhood difficult. Not everyone understands a little kid talking about creating my own Mydoom computer virus just for fun. My looks and ability to be a perfect young lady has kept my family on my side. My intelligence also helped our family wealth grow exponentially. Numbers are easy to me.

I stand at the periphery, a predator disguised as prey. My silver gray gown, a sheath of liquid silk, clings to every curve, its color a deliberate echo of his eyes. I adjust the pendant at my throat, an heirloom piece worth more than most people's homes. It's a calculated move, a subtle reminder of my lineage, my right to be here among the wolves in sheep's clothing. I glance down at the emerald ring on my finger. It's almost time.

My gaze cuts through the crowd like a scalpel, dissecting the scene with clinical precision. Every face is a mask, hiding desperation and greed behind champagne flutes and false smiles. I catalog each one, filing away weaknesses and potential leverage for future use. But they're not why I'm here. They're insignificant, mere obstacles between me and my true target.

And then I see him.

Hawk.

The air leaves my lungs in a rush as if I've been

struck. He stands tall and commanding in a perfectly tailored black suit, the stark lines emphasizing the breadth of his shoulders and the lean strength of his frame. Even from across the room, his presence is magnetic, drawing the eye and demanding attention.

He exudes danger from every pore. How could a man that magnetic even exist? The last time Hawk and I were in the same ballroom together is a night I will never forget.

A flurry of whispers ripples through the crowd as he moves, parting before him like the Red Sea. I drink in every detail, committing them to memory: the way his fingers curl around his glass, the subtle shift of muscle beneath his jacket as he turns, the sharp line of his jaw as he surveys the room with eyes the color of storm clouds.

Memories of my 18th birthday party flash unbidden through my mind. Hawk stepping in, his voice cold and cutting as he put Regina in her place, defending me from her vicious taunts. And afterward, my first time. It's been him and only him in my mind and heart. That day ignited something within me, a fascination that's only grown more intense with time. An obsession that's consumed my every waking moment for years.

I force myself to breathe, to maintain the calm facade I've spent years perfecting. I've learned a lot in the past six years. How to protect myself. How to speak up for myself. How to defend myself and be strong. But more than anything, how to take what I want. I take a breath again. But inside, I'm burning. Every cell in my body screams to go to him, to make him see me, recognize me. To claim what I've long since decided is mine.

Instead, I watch. I observe his interactions from afar, cataloging every subtle shift in his body language, every microexpression that crosses his face. The way his eyes narrow slightly when he's skeptical of what someone's saying. The almost imperceptible tightening of his jaw when he's annoyed but too polite to show it.

I've studied him for so long, I know his tells better than he does. His uncle and cousin try to get his attention, but I see him shut them down. His uncle's face pales and his cousin just stares at him in shock before they walk away. Poor bastards. Have they not realized there's a reason he's called the Devil?

A flash of red catches my eye, and I feel my entire body tense. Regina slinks up to Hawk, her blood-red gown a garish slash against the more muted tones around her. Her intentions are as transparent as the champagne in her glass—she leans in close, one manicured hand resting possessively on his arm.

Fury rises in me, hot and choking. That's my man she's touching. I visualize cutting off each of her fingers and feeding them to sharks. My hands itch to wrap around her throat, to tear her limb from limb for daring to touch what's mine. I take a sip of champagne to hide the snarl threatening to curl my lip, the delicate stem of the glass creaking in my white-knuckled grip.

But Hawk's response brings a wave of vicious satisfaction crashing over me. He shrugs off Regina's touch with a dismissal so cold it's practically glacial, leaving her standing alone and fuming. I savor her humiliation like a fine wine, letting it soothe the possessive rage still simmering beneath my skin.

As I relish Regina's defeat, the unthinkable happens. Hawk's steel-gray eyes lock onto mine from across the ballroom, and the world around us fades away. The cacophony of voices dulls to a distant hum as if I've been plunged underwater. Every detail sharpens with preternatural clarity—the clink of glasses, the rustle of silk, the faint notes of his cologne carried to me on an eddy of air. Does he remember the old me? I've changed from that innocent, shy girl. Can he see it?

For a moment, just a fraction of a second, I forget how to breathe. His gaze pins me in place, a butterfly on a board, exposed and vulnerable. I feel naked beneath the intensity of his stare as if he can see straight through the carefully constructed persona I present to the world, right down to the dark, obsessive core of me.

Recognition flashes across his face, quickly followed by something I can't quite identify—possession? curiosity? Before I can analyze it further, a guest intercepts him, shattering the moment. The spell breaks, sound and movement rushing back in a dizzying wave.

My heart pounds against my ribcage like a caged animal as I retreat behind a marble column, seeking refuge in the shadows. Does he truly recognize me after all these years? Is he expecting the old me? How will he react when he realizes I've changed? The thought sends a thrill of excitement coursing through me, followed quickly by a stab of panic. This isn't like me. I've learned a lot in six years. I'm always in control, always three steps ahead. Yet one look from Hawk has left me feeling exposed, my carefully laid plans teetering on the edge of chaos. Does he remember us?

I take a deep breath, forcing my racing thoughts into order. I need to recalibrate, to decide whether to make my presence known or continue observing from afar. The temptation to hack into the hotel's security feeds later tonight is strong—I could review every one of Hawk's interactions, dissecting each gesture and word until I've gleaned every possible scrap of information.

As I formulate my next move, movement near the bar catches my eye. Regina is speaking urgently to a waiter, her body language screaming of covert intentions. I watch as she slips something into a folded napkin, pressing it into the waiter's hand along with folded bills, giving him a meaningful look.

My eyes narrow, tracking the waiter's path through the crowd. He weaves between clusters of chattering guests, making a beeline for Hawk. Suspicion coils in my gut as I watch the waiter approach, presenting Hawk with a fresh drink on a silver tray.

Hawk takes the glass with a nod of thanks, bringing it to his lips. I lean forward, every muscle in my body tense as I watch him take a sip. For a moment, nothing happens. Then, almost imperceptibly, his confident posture begins to falter.

I watch, heart in my throat, as Hawk rubs his temple, blinking slowly. Confusion clouds his features, a furrow appears between his brows as he glances around the room. The realization hits me like a jolt of electricity: Regina has drugged him. My mind races through possibilities—a sedative? No, the way his pupils have dilated, the flush creeping up his neck... an aphrodisiac. She means to compromise him, to use his own body against him. Fucking bitch. She's truly despicable.

Time seems to slow as I weigh my options. Do I allow Regina's plan to unfold? Or do I intervene, protecting Hawk and potentially exposing myself in the process? The thought of letting her plan unfold makes me sick. Hawk is mine.

Regina sluices through the gathering toward him, ready to swoop in and take advantage of the opportunity.

The decision crystallizes in an instant, as clear and sharp as a diamond. I won't let Regina succeed, not when I've spent years cultivating my own carefully laid plans. Hawk Rivers is mine, and I'll be damned if I let that witch sink her claws into him.

I move swiftly through the crowd, my gown flowing around me like water. Guests part before me, sensing perhaps the predatory intent in my stride. I approach Hawk with measured steps, schooling my features into a mask of concern.

Several feet behind Hawk, Regina's eyes meet mine and she freezes, a scowl marring her expression. I continue forward, silently daring her to try to stop me.

"Mr. Rivers," I say, my voice steady and tinged with just the right amount of worry. "You don't look well. Let me help you." I offer my arm for support, meeting his unfocused gaze.

Hawk hesitates, and I see the struggle play out across his face. Even drugged, his instincts are sharp—he knows something isn't right. But the confusion wins out, and after a moment that feels like an eternity, he allows me to guide him.

The moment his hand closes around my arm, it's as if every nerve-ending in my body comes alive. His touch, even though the fabric of my gown, sends electricity arcing across my skin. I have to stifle a gasp, the intensity of my reaction catching me off guard. For years, I've dreamed of this moment, imagined what it would feel like to have Hawk depend on me, need me. The reality is so much more intoxicating than I could have ever anticipated.

Glancing back to see Regina glowering at us, I lead him toward a side door. Fuck, I missed him. I missed him so much. My 18th birthday party and our first night together replay in my mind like a constant reminder of what I've been waiting for. "Just a little farther," I murmur, my lips nearly brushing his ear. "I'm going to get you somewhere safe."

He turns his head slightly, his clouded gaze struggling to focus on me. "Is it you?"

A thrill runs through me at his words. Does he really recognize me? "It's me," I say softly, choosing my words carefully. "But that's not important right now. What matters is getting you out of here before anyone notices something's wrong."

We slip through the hotel side door and into the

service hallways beyond. The difference is stark—gone are the glittering chandeliers and marble floors, replaced by harsh fluorescent lighting and utilitarian tile. But I navigate these back corridors with the same confidence I showed in the ballroom, my extensive research of the hotel's layout paying off.

Hawk leans more heavily against me as we walk, the drug clearly taking a stronger hold. I tighten my grip on him, hyperaware of every point of contact between us. He's massive and I struggle to keep him from falling into me. The solid warmth of his body pressed against my side, the flex of muscle beneath my fingers as I guide him around a corner. It's almost more than I can bear, this sudden proximity after years of watching from afar.

"Where... where are we going?" Hawk mumbles, his words slightly slurred.

"Somewhere safe," I repeat, my voice low and soothing. "Just trust me, Hawk. You know you can trust me, right?"

He's silent for a long moment, and I wonder if he's even heard me. But then he nods, just once, and something fierce and possessive unfurls in my chest. He trusts me. Maybe it's just the drug, maybe it's desperation, but in this moment, Hawk has placed his faith in me. It's intoxicating.

As we near an exit, movement at the end of the

hallway catches my eye. Two men in dark suits, their stances screaming *security*, are scanning the area. I recognize them immediately as Regina's associates—no doubt waiting for Regina to arrive with a staggering Hawk in tow. Fuck. I can't let them take him.

My pulse quickens, but I maintain my composure, quickly diverting us down a back staircase. Hawk stumbles slightly on the first step, and I tighten my grip on his arm, supporting more of his weight.

"Careful," I murmur, guiding him down. "We're almost there. Just a little farther."

He nods, his jaw clenched with the effort of focusing on each step. Even drugged and vulnerable, there's a strength to him that takes my breath away. I want to stop and take his face in my hands and memorize every line and plane. To finally, finally touch him the way I've dreamed of for so long. I want to kiss him all over the place and bite my way down his body. The same way he did to mark me. But now isn't the time. We're not safe yet.

We emerge onto a quiet side street, the sounds of the city muffled and distant. I breathe a sigh of relief, quickly signaling to my driver. The sleek black sedan pulls up moments later, and I help Hawk into the back seat.

As I slide in beside him, I allow myself a small smile

of triumph. We made it. Against all odds, I've rescued Hawk from Regina's clutches, and now he's here alone with me. The possibilities make my head spin.

"I'm taking you home," I tell him, my tone leaving no room for argument. "You'll be safe there."

Hawk's head lolls against the leather headrest, his eyes half-closed. I study his profile in the passing streetlights, drinking in every detail. The strong line of his jaw, the curve of his lips, the faint shadow of stubble darkening his cheeks.

My fingers itch to trace the path my eyes are taking, to feel the heat of his skin beneath my touch. But I restrain myself, digging my nails into my palms. Now isn't the time for indulgence. I need to stay focused and maintain control of the situation.

"Why are you here?" Hawk's words are slightly slurred, but there's a sharpness beneath the confusion—a testament to his formidable will.

I consider my response carefully, weighing truth against fiction. "Because you need me," I say finally, my voice low and soothing. "Try to relax. We'll be at your home soon."

He struggles to focus on me, his brow furrowed in concentration. "Is it really you," he mumbles, reaching out to brush his fingers against my cheek.

His touch is like a brand, searing into my skin. I have

to stifle a gasp, every nerve ending lighting up at the contact. For a moment, I let myself lean into his hand, savoring the feeling I've fantasized about for so long. But then reality reasserts itself, and I gently pull away.

"Let's get you feeling better," I deflect, trying to ignore the way my skin tingles where he touched me. "For now, just rest."

Hawk's eyes drift closed, his breathing growing steadier. I allow myself to relax slightly, knowing we're out of immediate danger. But my mind is already racing ahead, plotting our next moves. Tonight has set new pieces in motion on the chessboard of our intertwined lives. And I intend to use every advantage to ensure I come out on top. Hawk needs me. It's why I'm back. To claim what's mine and to help him.

As the car weaves through the late-night traffic, I can't help but feel a surge of anticipation. I've imagined being alone with Hawk for years, scheming countless scenarios. But this—having him vulnerable and dependent on me—this is beyond anything I could have orchestrated. The possibilities make my pulse quicken and my skin flush with heat.

I reach into my clutch, retrieving a small device. With a few taps, I activate a series of protocols designed to scrub any footage of our exit from the hotel's security systems. It's a precaution I always take, but tonight it feels especially crucial. No one can know about this encounter, not until I decide how best to use it to my advantage.

The city lights blur outside the window as we near Hawk's building. I steel myself for what's to come, knowing that every word, every action from this point forward could shape the course of our future interactions. The game has changed, and I'm determined to emerge victorious.

As we pull up to the private entrance of Hawk's luxury high-rise, I take a deep breath. This is it—the moment I step fully into Hawk's world, crossing a threshold I've only observed through my hacking of his security until now. I turn to him, finding his eyes open but glazed.

"We're here, Mr. Rivers," I say softly, unable to keep a hint of excitement from creeping into my voice. "Let's get you inside."

He nods, attempting to straighten but swaying slightly. I exit the car first, then lean in to help him out. The moment my hands touch him again, it's like a circuit completing. Energy hums beneath my skin, and I have to force myself to focus on the task at hand rather than getting lost in the feeling.

The doorman rushes forward, concern evident on his face. "Mr. Rivers! Are you all right, sir?"

I intercept smoothly before Hawk can respond, stepping slightly in front of him in a protective stance. "Mr. Rivers isn't feeling well," I say, my voice smooth and authoritative. "I'm a family friend, just making sure he gets home safely." I flash a reassuring smile, projecting an air of calm confidence that leaves no room for question.

The doorman hesitates, clearly torn between his duty to assist and his suspicion of a stranger. I press on, my voice taking on a hint of steel. "I assure you, everything is fine. Mr. Rivers would appreciate discretion in this matter."

Something in my tone must convince him because he nods and steps back. "Of course. Let me know if you need any assistance."

I guide Hawk to the private elevator, keeping a steadying hand on his arm. As the doors slide closed, shutting us off from prying eyes, I feel a rush of exhilaration. We're alone now, truly alone in a space I've only seen through hacked security feeds. The air feels charged, electric with possibility.

Hawk leans heavily against the elevator wall, his breathing noticeably heavier. His eyes, when they meet mine, are a whirl of confusion and something darker, more primal. I watch as he clenches his fists, his jaw tight with the effort of maintaining control.

"You knew exactly where to go," he says, his words slightly slurred but his gaze intent. "How?"

I keep my expression neutral even as my heart races. He's fighting the drug's effects, but I can see the battle playing out across his face. I need to tread carefully. "I've attended events at the hotel before," I say smoothly. "The layout isn't difficult to remember."

He studies me for a long moment, and I can almost see him trying to piece together the puzzle I present. But then his eyes drop to my lips, lingering there before he wrenches his gaze away, swallowing hard.

He takes a step toward me, then stops abruptly as if afraid of what he might do if he gets too close.

I consider my response carefully, knowing I can't reveal too much. Instead, I deflect, turning the focus back to him. "How are you feeling? Any dizziness? Nausea?"

He blinks, momentarily thrown by the change in subject. "I'm... I'm not sure," he admits, his voice rough. He runs a hand through his hair, the movement drawing my eye to the flex of muscle beneath his shirt. "Everything feels... intense."

As we step into Hawk's penthouse, a thrill of triumph courses through me. Months of planning, of maneuvering myself back into my family's social circles, have led to this moment. My presence at the gala wasn't chance—it was the carefully orchestrated next step in my grand design. Regina's clumsy attempt at manipulation has only served to accelerate my plans, gifting me an opportunity I couldn't have dreamed of.

I guide Hawk to the large leather couch dominating the living area, savoring every point of contact between us. As he sinks into the cushions, I notice the sheen of sweat on his brow, the flush creeping up his neck. The drug is taking a stronger hold, and the sight sends a surge of excitement through me.

"Water," I murmur, more to myself than to him. "You need water."

I move to the kitchen, my steps sure and confident. As I fill a glass from the tap, I hear a sharp intake of breath behind me. I turn to find Hawk standing in the kitchen doorway, his eyes dark with undisguised want. The naked desire in his gaze makes my breath catch.

"Devin," he says, his voice low and rough.

He takes a step toward me, then another, until he's close enough that I feel the heat radiating off his body. The way he says my name makes me giddy. My heart races, a mix of anticipation and triumph surging through me. This is what I've wanted for so long—Hawk Rivers, the object of my obsession, looking at me like I'm the only thing in the world that matters.

"Mr. Rivers," I say, fighting to keep my voice steady. "You've been drugged. You need to drink this and rest."

I offer him the glass, but as he reaches for it, his fingers wrap around my wrist instead. The touch sends electricity arcing through me, and I can't stifle the small gasp that escapes me. Hawk's eyes darken at the sound.

"I don't want to rest," he murmurs, leaning in close. His breath ghosts across my cheek, sending shivers down my spine. "I want you. Fuck, I want you so much it hurts."

The raw need in his voice is intoxicating. I've dreamed of this for years, imagined countless scenarios where Hawk would look at me this way again. The reality is so much more intense, so much more exhilarating than anything I could have fantasized about.

"Mr. Rivers," I say softly, not pulling away despite knowing I should. "You're not yourself right now."

He laughs, a low, dark sound that sends heat pooling in my belly. "I've never felt more like myself," he says, his free hand coming up to cup my cheek.

I lean into his touch, unable to help myself. The feeling of his skin against mine is electric, addictive. For a moment, I let myself imagine giving in, taking what I've wanted for so long. But no—not like this. When I finally have Hawk Rivers, I want him fully aware, fully present.

With herculean effort, I gently extract myself from his grasp. "You need to rest," I tell him even as every fiber of my being screams to close the distance between us again.

Hawk's eyes narrow, a flash of his usual sharpness breaking through the drug's fog. "You're holding back," he accuses, following me as I retreat into the living room.

I back away, maintaining the illusion of propriety even as excitement thrums through me. This cat-and-mouse game, this dance of desire and restraint, is everything I've ever wanted. "No one ever tells everything, Mr. Rivers," I reply smoothly. "Especially not in our circles."

He stalks me across the room with a predatory grace that belies his intoxicated state. When my back hits the wall, he plants one hand beside my head, the other wrapping around my throat. The heat of him, the scent of his cologne mixed with the musk of his skin, is overwhelming.

FOUR

The city lights blur past the tinted windows of the sleek, black sedan as we approach my penthouse. Each flash of neon feels like a jolt to my drug-addled system, but I force my mind to remain sharp, focused on the woman beside me—Devin West. My Devin West.

I've missed her so fucking much. Seeing her again is like getting water after a drought. Dark hair cascades over her shoulders, framing a face I've dreamed about for years. Her striking green eyes, the same ones that have haunted me since her birthday party, now watch me with a mixture of concern and something darker, more intriguing.

As we pull up to the private entrance, I steel myself. The drug may be coursing through my veins, but I can't show my hand. Not now. Not when I finally have her within reach after all this time.

"We're here, Mr. Rivers," she says, her voice low and controlled. The sound of it sends a shiver down my spine. How many times have I imagined her saying my name? "Let me help you inside."

I nod, allowing her to assist me out of the car. I let my stride falter, playing up the drug's effects. Her arm slips around my waist, and the contact, even through layers of clothing, feels electric. Her grip tightens slightly, supporting me, and I have to stifle a groan at the feeling of her body pressed against mine.

"Careful," she murmurs, her breath warm against my ear. "Just a few more steps."

We approach the entrance, and to my surprise, Devin inputs the access code without hesitation. My security system is state-of-the-art, known only to a select few. Yet she navigates it with the ease of familiarity. Interesting. Very interesting. What other secrets are you hiding, Devin?

"Is it really you?" I ask, wanting to hear her speak.

"It's me."

The penthouse doors slide open silently, revealing the expansive living area beyond. Floor-to-ceiling windows offer a panoramic view of the city skyline, the lights twinkling like stars against the night sky. The space feels charged, alive with an electric tension that crackles between us.

I stumble, this time genuinely caught off guard by a wave of dizziness. "Sorry," I mutter, leaning more heavily on her. The scent of her perfume—something floral with an underlying musk—envelops me. "Everything's... spinning." It's an easy lie and perfect to keep her near me.

"You should sit down," she says, guiding me toward the leather couch. Her hand splays across my back, steadying me, and I swear I can feel the heat of her palm through my suit jacket. It takes every ounce of self-control not to lean into her touch, to demand more.

I watch through half-lidded eyes as she moves to the kitchen, retrieving a bottle of water. Each step is purposeful and confident, her hips swaying in a way that draws my gaze like a magnet. She navigates my space as if she knows it intimately, and the sight stirs something primal within me. This is not the fragile girl from six years ago. There's more to this Devin than meets the eye, and I'm determined to uncover every layer.

"Mr. Rivers," she says, her voice wavering slightly. "You've been drugged. You need to drink this and rest."

She offers me the glass, but as I reach for it, I let my fingers wrap around her wrist instead. The contact sends a jolt of electricity through me, and I have to stifle a groan. I hear a small gasp escape her lips, and the sound ignites something urgent within me.

I sense my eyes darken with desire, and I see the effect it has on her—the slight dilation of her pupils, the quickening of her breath. Fuck, how I've missed her. I don't want to think about how one night with her stopped me from wanting any other woman since. She's been the only person in my mind for six years.

"I don't want to rest," I murmur, leaning in close. I let my breath ghost across her cheek, reveling in the shiver that runs through her body. "I want you. Fuck, I want you so much it hurts."

The words aren't entirely an act. The drug may be amplifying my desires, but the want—the need—for Devin has been simmering for years. Now, with her so close, it's all I can do not to claim her right here, right now. I've been waiting for her. Now, I can have her.

"Mr. Rivers," she says softly, not pulling away despite the hesitation in her voice. "You're not yourself right now."

I laugh, a low, dark sound that I see sends a flush creeping up her neck. "I've never felt more like myself," I tell her, bringing my free hand up to cup her cheek. The softness of her skin under my palm is intoxicating, and I have to resist the urge to pull her closer.

She leans into my touch, her eyes fluttering closed for a moment. The sight of her, so responsive to my touch, so clearly wanting this as much as I do, nearly breaks my resolve. I want to take her right here, consequences be damned. This game we're playing is too delicious to end so soon.

With what seems like considerable effort, Devin extracts herself from my grasp. "You need to rest," she tells me, but I hear the strain in her voice and see the way her body unconsciously leans toward mine even as she steps away.

I narrow my eyes, letting a flash of my usual sharpness break through the drug's manufactured fog. "You're holding back," I accuse, following her as she retreats into the living room. Every step feels like I'm being pulled by an invisible thread, my body gravitating toward hers.

She backs away, but I can see the excitement thrumming through her, belying her attempt at propriety. "No one ever tells everything, Mr. Rivers," she replies smoothly. "Especially not in our circles."

Her words are a challenge, and I feel a thrill run through me. This cat-and-mouse game, this dance of desire and restraint, is everything I've ever wanted. We started this game six years ago and now we can finally play.

I stalk her across the room, my movements

purposeful despite my supposed intoxication. When her back hits the wall, I plant a hand next to her head and wrap the other around her throat, holding her still. I squeeze but she's not showing any fear.

The heat of her body, the scent of her perfume mixed with something uniquely her, is overwhelming. I lean in close, squeeze her throat, and brush my lips over her ear. "Tell me," I demand and bite on her earlobe. "Why, Devin," my voice is low and rough. "Why can't I get you out of my head."

I feel her shudder against me, and it takes every ounce of self-control not to press my body fully against hers. I pull back slightly, meeting her gaze. The desire I see there mixed with a calculated gleam that mirrors my own sends a rush of excitement through me.

For a moment, we're suspended in time, the air between us thick with tension and unspoken promises. Then, slowly, deliberately, I lower my head, my lips hovering just above hers. "Devin," I breathe, her name a prayer and a curse on my lips.

And then we're crashing together, all pretense abandoned. The kiss is fierce, hungry, years of pent-up desire unleashed in a single moment. Her hands tangle in my hair, pulling me closer, and I groan into her mouth. Her nails scrape at the back of my neck, leaving claw marks I can't help but love. My body presses her against the wall, every point of contact sending sparks of pleasure through me.

As we lose ourselves in each other, a small part of my mind remains alert, observing. The way Devin moves against me, the little sounds she makes—it's all filed away, pieces of a puzzle I'm determined to solve. Because even as I give in to this moment of passion, I know it's just the beginning.

Devin thinks she's the one in control, but she has no idea this has been a long time in the making. This is more than desire, more than obsession. When she looked at me with her innocent grateful eyes the night I took her virginity, she became mine. And I don't give away what belongs to me.

We finally break apart and she helps me back onto the sofa.

"Mr. Rivers," she says, her voice slightly strained. "You should rest."

I reach out, my fingers brushing against her hand. The contact sends sparks racing up my arm, and I have to bite back a groan. "Stay," I say, the single word laden with meaning. "I don't want to be alone."

She hesitates, and I can see the internal struggle playing out behind her eyes. For a moment, I think she might refuse. But then she nods slowly, sinking down beside me on the couch. "All right," she agrees, her voice barely above a whisper.

The air between us thickens even further, charged with unspoken tension. I can feel the heat radiating from her body and smell the subtle aroma of her natural scent. It's intoxicating in a way that has nothing to do with the drug in my system.

"Devin. My Devin." Will she admit to who she is? Admit to us?

Her eyes widen slightly, a mixture of caution and something darker—desire, perhaps?—swirling in their depths. "The drug is making you confused," she suggests, but there's an undercurrent to her words, a tension that belies her calm exterior.

"No," I insist, leaning closer. Our faces are inches apart now, and I can see the rapid pulse beating at the base of her throat. "I know you're my Devin."

For a moment, we're suspended in time, balanced on the knife's edge between restraint and abandon. I can see the war raging behind her eyes, the same battle I'm fighting within myself. Then, as if a switch has been flipped, we're crashing together.

And once again, all control is gone. Our lips meet in a fervent kiss that ignites every nerve ending in my body. It's like a dam breaking, the earlier kiss only laid the foundation for this one. Devin responds with equal passion, her fingers tangling in my hair, and her moans making me so hard, I can barely think. She pulls me closer, her nails digging at the back of my neck. I growl low in my throat, the sound more animal than human.

"Devin," I breathe against her lips, tasting her name like a forbidden fruit.

Grabbing her by the arm, I drag her toward my bedroom but she stops me by the walls just a few steps away from the sofa. Without a word, I grip her throat, my fingers wrapping around her delicate neck. She stumbles, her hands clawing at mine, but I don't let go.

I shove her against the wall, my body pressing against hers. Her breath hitches, her eyes flashing with anger and something else. Something darker. Something that calls to the devil inside me.

"What's wrong, sweetheart?" I murmur, my voice low and dangerous. She squirms, trying to break free, but I hold her tightly, my grip unyielding. "Don't you want this?"

"You're drugged. Let me go," she hisses.

I laugh. "Never," I growl, my free hand shoving the skirt on her dress up and bunching it at her waist. Then I yank down her thong, exposing her to me. I run my hand through her slick folds, a smirk playing on my lips as I feel her wetness. "Look how wet you are for me. Your body knows who it belongs to."

She tries to fight me, her hands pushing against my chest, her legs kicking out. But I'm stronger. I always have been. I slip a finger inside her, then another, my thumb circling her clit.

She gasps, her body tensing, her eyes filled with a mix of anger and desire. "You're going to have to fight harder," I murmur, my voice thick with lust. "Otherwise, I'm going to make you come all over my hand right here."

I continue to finger fuck her, my hand moving in a steady rhythm, my thumb applying just the right amount of pressure. And between my words and my ministrations, she finally gives in.

She melts against me, her body softening, her breath coming in short gasps. I lean in, my lips brushing against her ear. "That's it, sweetheart," I growl. "Give in to it. Give in to me."

She comes with a cry, her body convulsing, her pussy clenching around my fingers. I hold her tightly, my hand still around her throat, my body pressing against hers. She's mine. She's always been mine.

And now that I have her again, I'm never letting her go. Not again. Not ever.

I reach down with one hand, undoing my pants, freeing my cock. Devin's eyes widen, her body tensing, and she starts to fight again. She pushes against my chest, her legs kicking out, trying to dislodge me. "You're not in your right mind."

I laugh, a harsh, mocking sound. "This act is pointless," I growl, my hand gripping her thigh, feeling the slickness of her arousal. "Your thighs are soaked. You want this. You want me. So just part those pretty legs and let me in."

Her eyes flash with defiance, her nails digging into my arms. I smirk, wrapping her legs around my waist and positioning myself at her entrance. With one swift thrust, I slam into her, burying myself deep inside her tight, wet heat.

She yelps, her body jerking, her hands coming up to grip my shoulders, her nails digging in so hard, I can feel the sting. I bare my teeth at her, a feral grin, as I feel the trickle of blood.

She's marked me. Good. I want her to. I want her to leave her claim on me, just like I'm leaving mine on her.

I pin her against the wall, my hips moving in a relentless rhythm, my cock sliding in and out of her. She fights me, her body bucking against mine. I hiss at how fucking good she feels squeezing around me, my grip on her tightening as I continue to fuck her, our bodies locked in a battle of wills.

"You feel that?" I groan, my voice thick with lust. "You feel how fucking hard you make me?" I slam in even harder, and she moans, her head falling back against the wall, her eyes glazed with desire. "Oh, fuck, I love the way you squeeze my cock."

Her hips start to move in sync with mine, her body meeting my thrusts, her pussy clenching around my shaft. I lean in, my lips brushing against her ear, my voice a low growl. "This pussy is mine. You can fight it all you want, but you know it's true. You know no one can make you feel like this."

I know she remembers me. I know she understands I'm not talking about just now.

She twists so her mouth is at my neck, her teeth sinking into my flesh. I hiss, my hips moving faster, my cock pounding into her with a force that leaves us both breathless.

I feel her orgasm building, her body tensing, her breath coming in short gasps. My own release approaches, my cock swelling inside her, my balls tightening.

"Come with me," I growl, my voice thick with need. "Prove to me how much you love the way I fuck you."

She cries out, her body convulsing, her pussy clenching around my cock as she comes. I groan, my own orgasm hitting me like a freight train, my cock pulsing as I fill her with my come. We ride out our pleasure together, our bodies locked in a fierce embrace, our breaths mingling, our hearts pounding in sync.

As we come down from our high, I press my forehead against hers, my eyes locked onto hers. She stares at me, her eyes filled with a mix of anger, desire, and resignation. There's no denying what she wants to ignore.

She's mine.

Afterward, as we lie tangled together on the couch, I feel the weight of exhaustion settling in. The drug's lingering effects pull at my consciousness, but I fight it, not wanting this moment to end.

"Rest now," she murmurs, her voice soft and soothing. She adjusts a pillow beneath my head, and for a brief moment, I see a flash of vulnerability in her expression. It's gone so quickly, I almost think I imagined it, but it sears itself into my memory.

As my eyes drift closed, satisfaction washes over me. Devin West is finally here, in my arms, exactly where I've wanted her for so long. The feel of her body against mine, the scent of her on my skin—it's everything I've dreamed of and more.

My last conscious thought before sleep claims me is a promise to myself: I will unlock every one of Devin's secrets, no matter what it takes. She is mine now, and I have no intention of ever letting her go.

I WAKE to the soft glow of dawn filtering through the floor-to-ceiling windows, my head pounding with the aftereffects of whatever I was drugged with. For a moment, I'm disoriented, the events of the previous night feeling like a vivid dream. But then the memories come rushing back in a flood of sensory detail—Devin's touch, her taste, the way she moved against me. My body responds instantly to the recollection, desire coursing through me anew.

But as I sit up, the cool air hitting my bare skin, I realize I'm alone. The penthouse is silent, no trace of her presence save for the lingering scent of her perfume on the couch cushions. I bring the fabric to my nose, inhaling deeply, trying to recapture the essence of her.

A rueful smile tugs on my lips. Of course, she left. Devin isn't one to linger for morning-after pleasantries. I could tell the moment our gazes met at the gala that she wasn't the scared little eighteen-year-old I saved from Regina.

There was control and something else in her eyes. I've finally gotten her back in my grasp. But now that I've had a taste, the need for more gnaws at me with an intensity that's almost frightening.

I stand, stretching out the kinks in my muscles, and

make my way to the kitchen. As I pour myself a much-needed cup of coffee, my mind races, analyzing every moment of our encounter. Each touch, bite, and kiss plays on a loop in my head, stoking the fire of my obsession.

Devin's confidence in my home, her familiarity with my security system, the way she seemed to know my body so intimately. She's been watching me, studying me, just as I've been watching her. The thought sends a thrill of excitement through me. We're more alike than I ever imagined, and it only makes me want her more.

I take a sip of coffee, savoring the bitter taste as I gaze out at the city sprawled below. The sun is rising, painting the sky in shades of pink and gold, but all I can think about is the green of Devin's eyes, the softness of her skin.

Whatever Devin's motivations, one thing is clear: the game has changed. The lines between us have blurred irrevocably, and I find myself more intrigued—more obsessed—than ever. Last night was just the beginning, a taste of what could be. And now that I've had that taste, I know I'll never be satisfied until I have all of her.

A ping from my phone draws my attention. It's a message from Daniel, my right-hand man: "Unusual activity detected in our systems overnight. Possible breach attempt. Need to discuss."

Interesting timing. Could this be connected to Devin's sudden reappearance in my life? The possibility sends another thrill of excitement through me. Perhaps there's more to her than I ever imagined. The thought of Devin as not just an object of desire, but a worthy opponent in every arena, makes my pulse quicken.

I type out a quick response to Daniel, then set my coffee cup down with a decisive click. Time to get to work. There are mysteries to unravel, pieces to put into place. And at the center of it all, Devin West.

My fingers trace the edge of the couch where we lay entwined just hours ago. The memory of her body against mine, the sound of her gasps and moans, fuels a fire in my veins. Devin thinks she can play me? She has no idea what she's awakened.

I've been waiting years for this dance to begin, and I intend to lead. Every step and every turn will bring her closer to me, deeper into the web of desire and obsession I've been weaving since the moment I first laid eyes on her.

FIVE

The soft hiss of the apartment door sliding shut behind me echoes in the dimly lit space. I step into my sanctuary, my technological haven. The glow of multiple monitors casts an eerie blue hue across the room, illuminating the stark contrast between this space and Hawk's minimalist penthouse. Wires snake along the floor like cybernetic vines, and the quiet hum of servers provides a comforting white noise.

I toss my clutch onto a nearby chair, the metallic clank of its chain strap against the leather seat punctuating the silence. My mind is already racing, replaying every moment of last night with Hawk Rivers. The weight of the encounter sits heavy in my chest, a mix of exhilaration and unease that I can't quite shake.

I sink into my ergonomic chair, the familiar contours cradling me as I pull up the surveillance footage from Hawk's penthouse on one of the main screens. The crystal-clear image flickers to life, and I'm transported back to that moment.

My eyes fixate on the video, watching our intimate encounter unfold. I study Hawk's expressions, the subtle shifts in his body language. The way his stormy gray eyes darken with desire, the twitch of his jaw as he restrains himself, the precise movements of his hands as they explore my body. Each replay intensifies the obsession coiling tighter within me, a serpent winding around my heart.

I pause on a frame where Hawk's eyes reflect a potent mix of desire and cunning. My fingers trace his face on the screen, leaving smudges on the glossy surface.

"What are you hiding, Hawk?" I murmur, leaning in closer as if proximity might reveal his secrets. The scent of his cologne, a heady mix of sandalwood and something uniquely him, lingers in my memory.

The encrypted line on my secure phone chirps, breaking my trance. It's Max, my trusted assistant and fellow hacker. His voice comes through, clear and professional.

"Devin, we've got an interesting development. Rivers Financial has reached out to Sphinx via the dark web."

My pulse quickens, a flutter beneath my skin. "What do they want?"

"They're requesting Sphinx's help to restore video footage from the gala," Max explains, a hint of curiosity in his tone. "Apparently, someone scrubbed the surveillance feeds."

A smirk spreads on my face, the irony delicious on my tongue. Of course, I was the one who erased that footage, intending to keep evidence against Regina Black for future leverage. The thought of Hawk seeking my alter ego's help sends a thrill through me.

"Interesting," I muse, mind already spinning with possibilities. My fingers dance across the keyboard, pulling up encrypted files. "Max, I want you to respond with a proposition."

"What do you have in mind?"

I pause for dramatic effect, savoring the moment. "Tell them Sphinx will restore the footage... if Hawk agrees to have a one-night stand with Sphinx."

There's a beat of silence on the other end, heavy with unspoken concerns. "Are you sure about this?" Max's voice carries a note of worry. "It's a bold move,

Devin. I mean, Rivers is the last person you should send that type of proposition to. We're treading dangerous waters here."

"Trust me," I reply, confidence lacing my words. My eyes flick to a framed photograph on the wall – a cityscape at night, lights blurring into streaks of color. It reminds me of the rush I feel when I'm in control. "I want to see how he reacts. Sometimes you have to make waves to see what surfaces."

I can almost hear Max's hesitation through the line, but he doesn't argue further. "All right, I'll send the message. But be careful, Devin. Men like Hawk Rivers don't take kindly to being played."

As I wait for a response, I feel the adrenaline coursing through my veins, electric and intoxicating. This game with Hawk is addictive, and I'm eager to see his next move.

Minutes later, Max's voice comes through again, this time tinged with something akin to disappointment. "Hawk's assistant responded. They said the terms are unacceptable and that Hawk...has someone. He's...um... not available."

"He has someone?" I repeat, the words tasting bitter on my tongue. Irritation creeps into my voice, and I can feel a spark of jealousy igniting in my chest. The idea that Hawk might be interested in someone else, that there might be another player in this game I didn't account for, is unacceptable. "What exactly did they say, Max?"

"The exact words were: 'Mr. Rivers is not available for such arrangements. He has someone in his life already. Your terms are unacceptable. If you wish to negotiate a standard contract for your services, please contact our legal department. We are willing to pay top dollar.'"

Without a second thought, I launch into a hacking frenzy. My fingers fly across the keyboard, the rapid-fire clicks filling the room. Lines of code scroll across the screen as I bypass layers of security to access Hawk's personal and business communications. Emails, messages, call logs – I comb through them all, searching for any hint of another woman, another connection. Who would dare to touch my man?

But as the minutes turn to hours, frustration mounts. There's nothing. No evidence of any significant female presence in Hawk's life beyond professional interactions. The lack of information is both a relief and a new source of anxiety.

"Who are you hiding, Hawk?" I mutter, eyes scanning line after line of data. The blue light from the screens casts harsh shadows across my face, reflected in the darkened window beside me.

Despite the fruitless search, my mind keeps circling back to the previous night. The way Hawk looked at me, the intensity of our connection. I replay snippets of our conversation in my head, analyzing every word, every gesture for hidden meanings.

"So beautiful," he had said, his voice low and husky. The memory of his breath against my ear sends a shiver down my spine.

The line between professional detachment and personal obsession blurs further with each passing moment. I'm losing myself in this, and a small part of me knows it's dangerous. But the thrill is too potent to resist.

Suddenly, my personal phone rings, cutting through my concentration. I recognize the number instantly – Hawk's private line. My heart rate spikes, and I hesitate before answering, composing myself.

"Devin," Hawk's smooth voice comes through, masking any underlying intentions. There's a richness to his tone that makes my name sound like a caress. "Let's meet up."

I suppress a smile, relishing the subtle power I hold in this moment. "I'm afraid I'm busy, Hawk," I respond coolly, forcing nonchalance into my voice. "Perhaps another time."

"Are you sure?" There's a hint of challenge in his words.

The temptation to agree is strong, but I resist. "Another time, Hawk. Have a good evening."

After ending the call, a surge of satisfaction washes over me. Holding the upper hand with Hawk, even in this small way, is exhilarating. I contemplate the dynamics of our relationship – both of us maneuvering for control, each hiding secrets from the other.

"Let's see how badly you want to see me," I whisper to the empty room, already planning my next move. The city lights twinkle beyond my window, a constellation of possibilities.

The decision crystallizes in my mind. I'll visit the underground pleasure den Hawk owns. It's a place where identities are concealed and I can observe him without pretense. I select my disguise with care – a sleek, black mask that will hide my features, its surface adorned with intricate silver filigree. My outfit is a study in elegance and allure – a deep crimson dress that clings to my curves, with a daring slit up one thigh. It's designed to draw attention while maintaining anonymity.

As I prepare, I equip myself with hidden devices. A small earpiece, nearly invisible, connects me to Max for real-time updates. A discreet camera no larger than a pinhead is embedded in the intricate design of my necklace, ready to capture anything of interest. And, of course, my emerald ring I never take off.

"Max," I speak into the comm as I apply a final touch of deep red lipstick, "Get me more details on the attack on Rivers financial. I want to know who keeps trying to take them down. Also, I need you to monitor Hawk's movements. Alert me the moment he arrives at the den."

"Understood," Max replies, his tone neutral but I can sense his unease. "Devin, you're playing a dangerous game here. These people... they're not to be trifled with. Hawk isn't like a regular guy. He's ruthless. You know this."

I dismiss his caution with a wave of my hand, even though he can't see it. The cool metal of my bracelet slides against my wrist, a reminder of the barriers I keep between myself and the world. "I know what I'm doing, Max."

As I leave my apartment, a mix of anticipation and apprehension swirls within me. The addictive pull of my obsession guides my actions, drowning out the small voice of reason that warns me of the risks. The night air is crisp against my skin as I slide into the waiting car, the city lights blurring as we speed toward the den.

The pleasure den's concealed entrance is hidden

behind an innocuous storefront. I approach, my heels clicking against the pavement, and murmur the password to the stone-faced guard. The door slides open, revealing a world of shadows and secrets.

I step inside, and the atmosphere envelops me like a velvet glove. Dim lighting casts everything in a sensual glow, and the air is thick with the scent of expensive perfumes, aged whiskey, and an underlying current of desire. The murmur of hushed conversations and soft, sensual music creates a cocoon of hedonistic indulgence.

I move gracefully through the crowd, my senses heightened as I search for any sign of Hawk. Bodies press close in the narrow corridors, a tangle of silk, leather, and bare skin. I observe it all with detached interest, noting the play of power and submission that unfolds around me.

A woman in a golden mask giggles as she's led away by two men in matching black suits. In a darkened alcove, I glimpse a scene of elaborate rope work, the bound submissive arching in ecstasy. It's all so predictable, so mundane. None of it stirs anything within me.

I settle at a secluded corner table, the plush velvet of the seat cool against my skin. A waitress clad in little more than strategically placed strips of leather approaches.

"What's your pleasure tonight?" she purrs, leaning in close.

"Scotch, neat," I reply, my tone neutral. Her proximity, meant to entice, leaves me cold.

As I wait, sipping my drink, my eyes never stop scanning the room, alert for Hawk's arrival. The amber liquid burns a path down my throat, but it's nothing compared to the fire Hawk ignites within me. The thrill of the game invigorates me, pushing aside any doubts or fears.

A man approaches my table, his mask adorned with peacock feathers. There's a confidence in his stride that speaks of wealth and influence. As he draws closer, I recognize him as James Holbrook, one of Hawk's business associates.

"Good evening, beautiful," he says, his voice smooth as silk. "I couldn't help but notice you sitting here all alone. Care for some company?"

I regard him coolly, taking in the expensive cut of his suit, the glint of his Rolex in the low light. "I'm quite comfortable as I am, thank you."

He's undeterred, sliding into the seat opposite me and reaching out to touch my wrist. "Come now, surely you didn't come to a place like this to sit alone. I have a private room upstairs... I could show you pleasures you've never dreamed of."

A sardonic smile plays at my lips. If only he knew the depths of my dreams, the complexity of my desires. "I appreciate the offer, Mr. Holbrook, but I'm not interested."

His eyes widen slightly behind his mask. "You know who I am?"

"I make it my business to know many things," I reply, taking another sip of my scotch. "Now, if you'll excuse me, I prefer my own company."

James opens his mouth to respond, but his words die on his lips as a hush falls over our corner of the room. I feel it before I see it – a shift in the air, a prickling awareness along my skin.

Hawk.

He moves through the crowd like a shark through water, people instinctively parting before him. His mask is simple but elegant, black leather that accentuates the sharp lines of his jaw. Our eyes meet across the room, and even from this distance, I can feel the intensity of his gaze.

His gaze shoots to where James is touching my wrist.

James, sensing the shift in power, stands quickly. "Raptor," he says, his tone full of nervousness. "I didn't realize you'd be here tonight."

Hawk doesn't even spare him a glance. His eyes are locked on me, a predatory gleam in their depths. "Leave us, James," he commands, his voice brooking no argument.

As James scurries away, Hawk approaches my table. The air between us crackles with tension with unspoken challenges and barely restrained desire.

SIX

The discreet entrance of the Pleasure Den looms before me, a portal to a world of shadows and secrets. I adjust my cufflinks, a subtle gesture of control before I step into the realm where control is both currency and illusion. The doorman, a stone-faced sentinel, nods imperceptibly as I approach. No words are necessary; my presence here is expected, anticipated.

As I descend the dimly lit staircase, I feel the weight of the mask in my hand. Sleek, black, with minimal embellishments – a reflection of my own carefully cultivated image. I place it over my face, feeling the cool leather against my skin. It's a second skin, really, another layer of the armor I wear every day.

The Den unfolds before me, a tapestry of opulence

and mystery. Candlelight flickers, casting dancing shadows on ornate walls. The air is thick with the scent of exotic spices and top-shelf liquor, a heady mix that speaks of indulgence and excess. Soft jazz mingles with electronic beats, creating an otherworldly ambiance that sets my nerves on edge.

My eyes scan the room, taking in the masked figures that glide through the space like specters. But they're all irrelevant, mere background noise. I'm here for one person, and one person only. Devin. The woman who's become an obsession, a riddle I'm determined to solve. My sources confirmed her presence, but in this sea of anonymity, finding her will be its own game.

I move through the crowd, my senses hyperaware. Every brush of fabric, every murmured conversation could be a clue. A woman in a zebra mask sidles up to me, her hand trailing along my arm.

"Looking for company tonight, handsome?" she purrs, her voice dripping with invitation.

I don't even spare her a glance. "No," I reply, my tone cold and final. She recoils as if slapped, melting back into the crowd.

Then, across the room, I see her. Even behind the delicate black mask adorned with intricate silver filigree, her presence is unmistakable. Devin moves with a confidence that sets her apart, her lithe form draped in a dress that seems to shimmer with every movement. The deep crimson fabric clings to her curves, the slit up one thigh offering tantalizing glimpses of skin with each step.

A familiar surge of desire wells up inside me, hot and urgent. My body responds instantly, a primal reaction I can barely control. I want to cross the room, to claim her in front of everyone. To let everyone know she's mine. But I tamp down the urge. We're playing a game of shadows and whispers tonight, and I intend to savor every moment.

She's in her element here, and it's intoxicating to witness. But then, a disruption. James Holbrook, a long-time business associate I've never particularly liked, approaches her. His body language is unmistakable – the slight lean in, the too-wide smile visible even beneath his gaudy gold mask. His hand reaches out, touching her wrist.

White-hot rage flares in my chest, consuming me. Holbrook is a known womanizer, and the sight of his hands on Devin makes me want to tear him limb from limb. I imagine the satisfying crunch of his bones breaking under my hands, the way his eyes would widen in terror as he realized his fatal mistake. It takes every ounce of control not to storm over and end him right there.

But I force myself to wait, to observe. This is a test – for her, for me, for us.

Devin's reaction is perfect. She's polite but distant, her body angled away from Holbrook in a subtle rejection. I hear her cool reply, "I make it my business to know many things. Now, if you'll excuse me, I prefer my own company." Pride mingles with my possessiveness. She's not interested in his advances, but the very fact that he dared approach her, touch her, makes my blood boil.

It's time to intervene.

I move through the crowd like a predator stalking its prey, people instinctively parting before me. My eyes are locked on Devin, a hunger I can barely contain burning within me. As I approach, a hush falls over our corner of the room. I feel the shift in the air, the prickling awareness that spreads through the gathered guests.

Holbrook opens his mouth to speak, but his words die on his lips as he notices me. Recognition flashes in his eyes as he takes in my mask. He knows who I am, even if he doesn't know why I'm here. Good. Let him feel the fear.

"Raptor," he says, his tone full of nervousness. "I didn't realize you'd be here tonight."

I don't even spare him a glance. My eyes are fixed on Devin, drinking in every detail of her. A predatory gleam burns in my gaze as I command, "Leave us, James."

As Holbrook scurries away like the insect he is, I approach Devin's table. The air between us crackles with tension, unspoken challenges, and barely restrained desire.

I extend my hand, falling easily into the charade. "It's rare to see new faces here. I'm Raptor."

Her hand slides into mine, cool and soft. The touch sends electricity racing up my arm.

"Silver," she responds, playing along seamlessly.

The irony of the moment isn't lost on me. We both know exactly who the other is, yet we dance this delicate dance of pretense. It's exhilarating.

"Care to dance?" I offer my arm, curious to see if she'll accept.

There's a moment of hesitation – real or feigned, I can't be sure – before she places her hand in the crook of my elbow. "Lead the way."

On the dance floor, our bodies move in perfect synchronicity. It's as if we've done this a thousand times before, which, in a way, we have. Every encounter, every subtle manipulation has been its own kind of dance. But this... this is different. The heat of her body so close to mine, the scent of her perfume – something exotic and spicy – filling my senses. It takes every ounce of control not to pull her flush against me.

"You move with confidence," I observe, my voice low, rough with barely contained desire. "Have you been here before?"

Her eyes glitter behind her mask, a mix of mischief and challenge. "Perhaps. I think these gatherings can be stimulating."

The way her lips form around the word *stimulating* sends a jolt straight to my groin. "Stimulating can be dangerous in the wrong company," I counter, my hand tightening slightly on her waist.

"Then I suppose I should choose my company wisely." Her breath ghosts across my ear as she leans in, her body pressing against mine for a brief, maddening moment.

As we move across the floor, I'm acutely aware of every point of contact between us. Her hand in mine, the pressure of her waist against my palm, the occasional brush of her thigh against mine. It's familiar yet thrillingly new in this context.

"You seem familiar," I remark, echoing an earlier sentiment but with deeper implication. My thumb traces small circles on her lower back, just above the curve of her ass.

"Do I?" Her tone is light, playful even, but I can

hear the slight catch in her breath. "Perhaps we crossed paths in another life. One where we were... intimately acquainted."

The tension between us builds with every exchange, every touch. Each word is a move in our private game of chess, neither of us willing to concede an inch. I find myself both frustrated and aroused by her ability to match me step for step.

As the music fades, I gesture toward a secluded alcove. "Would you care to continue our conversation somewhere more private?"

She tilts her head, considering. "And what would we discuss away from prying eyes?"

I lean in close, my lips barely brushing the shell of her ear. "All the ways I want to make you scream, Silver."

A visible shiver runs through her, and for a moment, I think I've won. But then she pulls back, a wicked smile playing at the corners of her mouth. "Promises, promises. But can you deliver... Raptor?"

She accepts with a nod, and I guide her to a private lounge area, my hand on the small of her back. Rich, dark fabrics surround us, creating a cocoon of intimacy. We sit opposite each other, the space between us charged with unspoken intentions.

"So, Silver," I begin, leaning forward slightly, my

eyes never leaving hers, "what really brings you to places like this? The thrill of anonymity? Or something more... primal?"

"Perhaps a bit of both," she answers, crossing her legs slowly, deliberately. The movement causes the slit in her dress to part, revealing a tantalizing expanse of thigh. "It's liberating to be whoever you wish, to indulge in desires you might otherwise keep hidden. Don't you think?"

"Indeed," I agree, my voice dropping to a near growl. "Though sometimes, masks conceal more than just faces. They hide our deepest, darkest wants."

"And what are your deepest, darkest wants... Raptor?" The way she says my pseudonym is like a caress.

I lean in closer, close enough to feel the heat radiating off her skin. "To peel away every layer of mystery surrounding you. To uncover every secret, every hidden desire. To make you come apart under my hands and mouth until you forget every name but mine."

Her breath hitches, a flush creeping up her neck. "Bold words. But actions speak louder, don't they?"

"Then let me show you," I murmur, reaching out to trace the line of her jaw with my fingertips.

THE PRIVATE ROOM I enter is dimly lit, the air thick with a heady mix of anticipation and desire. He follows me in and I sense his eyes on me, piercing and intense, even through the mask he wears. I'd know those eyes anywhere. Gray, like a raging sea, cold and calculating, yet burning with a hidden intensity.

He gives me one of those grins that never quite reaches his eyes, his voice a low rumble as he commands, "Crawl to me, sweetheart."

I should resist, but I didn't come in here to resist. I came here for him. Just like the first time, I find myself sinking to the floor, my hands and knees pressing into the cold, hard surface.

I crawl to him, my ass swaying with each movement, my body already responding to his commands. I come to rest before him, sitting on my knees, my eyes locked onto his as I stare up at him.

He unbuttons his shirt, letting it fall open and I notice something new on his chest. A tattoo he didn't have before. A black snake curled around a moth. It's the same tattoo I have, except his is much larger. I meet his gaze and stare. What does this mean? I want to ask him, but the way he's looking at me makes me hold the question in and focus on the moment. There's something else I want more.

He reaches out, his thumb brushing harshly over my

mouth, his touch sending a jolt of electricity straight to my core. "You look so fucking good like this," he murmurs, his voice thick with lust.

His words make me wet, my body responding to him in a way that it astounds me. He must see the blush on my cheeks, the desire in my eyes, because his gaze sharpens, turning hungrier. "Are you wet for me, Silver?" he asks, his voice a low growl.

I nod, my breath hitching as I press my thighs together, trying to ease the ache between them. He chuckles, a dark, dangerous sound as he points to a piece of furniture across the room. It's a bench of sorts, padded and shaped for one purpose only. "Go bend over that for me," he orders, his voice leaving no room for argument. "Ass in the air, legs spread. I want to see that wet pussy."

I hesitate for a moment, my body trembling with a mix of anticipation and nerves. But the desire in his eyes and the hunger in his voice has me complying. I stand, my legs shaking slightly as I make my way to the bench.

I bend over it, my ass in the air, my legs spread wide, exposing myself to him completely. His eyes burn me, his gaze like a physical touch as he takes in every inch of me. I hear him move behind me, his footsteps echoing in the dimly lit room. He slides my underwear out of the way, his fingers delving through my folds, groaning at the wetness he finds there.

"Fuck, you're soaked," he murmurs, his voice thick with lust. I hear rustling behind me and turn to see him rubbing my slickness over his length, stroking himself as he stares at my pussy. His eyes are dark, hungry, filled with a desire that borders on obsession. "I can't wait to have you," he growls, his voice sending a shiver down my spine.

He presses the head of his cock to my tight entrance, and I have just enough time to brace myself before he slams into me, stealing my breath. I scream, the sound echoing through the room as he fills me, stretches me. His cock is so big it's hard to adjust. He grunts, his fingers tangling in my hair, bowing my back as he starts to move, his hips thrusting against me in a punishing rhythm.

"Fuck, you're tight," he groans, his voice a low growl.

He pinches my nipple, the sharp pain making me clench around him. He chuckles, a dark, dangerous sound as he slaps my breast, the sting sending another wave of pleasure through me.

"You like that, don't you?" he murmurs, his voice thick with lust.

His words turn me on even more. My orgasm builds, my body tensing, my breath coming in short gasps.

He leans over me, his lips brushing against my ear, his voice a low growl. "I'm going to pump you so full of my cum, you'll never get me out. You'll be dripping with me."

His words push me over the edge, and I come with a cry, my body convulsing, my pussy clenching around his cock. He groans, his hips moving faster, pounding into me with a force that leaves me breathless. Just as I start to come down from my high, he pulls out, flipping me over onto my back.

He looms over me, his eyes dark, his breath coming in ragged gasps. "I can't wait to fill you over and over," he growls, his voice thick with need. "I can't wait to turn you into a begging, crying mess. And even then, I won't stop. I'll keep fucking you, keep filling you until you can't take anymore. Until you're completely and utterly mine."

His words send a shiver of anticipation and fear through me. I know he means it. I know he won't stop until he's claimed every inch of me, until he's filled me with every drop of his cum.

And as he slides back into me, his cock filling me once again, I know that I'm his. Completely and utterly his. And I can't wait for him to ruin me.

SEVEN

The Pleasure Den thrums with a palpable energy, a living, breathing entity of desire and secrets. I adjust my silver mask, feeling the cool metal against my flushed skin. The delicate filigree design allows me to observe without being truly seen, a metaphor for my life that isn't lost on me.

I weave through the crowd, my black dress a second skin, hugging every curve. The silk whispers against my thighs with each step, a constant reminder of my vulnerability and power. Eyes follow me—I feel their heat, their hunger—but I'm searching for only one gaze.

There. Across the room, leaning against the bar with predatory grace. Even with the black raptor mask obscuring half his face, I'd recognize him anywhere. Hawk. Or "Raptor," as he's known here. My pulse quickens, desire and adrenaline flooding my system in equal measure.

Our eyes lock, and the rest of the world fades away. He straightens, his broad shoulders pulling the fabric of his tailored shirt taut across his chest. I allow myself a moment to appreciate the view, knowing he's doing the same to me.

I approach slowly, deliberately. This is a dance we've perfected over the past few weeks, a delicate balance of seduction and restraint. Neither of us has acknowledged our true identities, reveling instead in the thrill of our shared secret.

"Silver," he greets me, his voice a low rumble that sends shivers down my spine. "I was beginning to think you wouldn't grace us with your presence tonight."

I quirk an eyebrow behind my mask. "Miss me, Raptor?"

His laugh is dark honey, rich and intoxicating. "Always. No one else here can match your... intensity."

He gestures to the bartender, who slides two glasses of deep red wine toward us. I take mine, letting my fingers brush against his. Even that slight contact sets my nerves alight.

"Merlot," I note, taking a sip. "Bold choice."

Raptor leans in, his breath hot against my ear. "I'm in a bold mood tonight."

I turn my head slightly, our lips a whisper apart. "Is that so? And what brought that on?"

His hand finds the small of my back, fingers splaying possessively. "You. Always you, Silver. The way you move, the way you smell..." He inhales deeply, nuzzling the spot just below my ear. "You've changed your perfume. Jasmine and... something darker. Intoxicating."

Pride and desire war within me. I've left him little hints throughout the week—a black rose delivered to his office, a cryptic note slipped to him at his favorite restaurant. The fact that he's noticed the perfume, a custom blend I had created just for tonight, sends a thrill through me.

"I like to keep things interesting," I murmur, allowing myself to lean into his touch.

"Oh, you never fail at that." His other hand comes to rest on my hip, and he pulls me flush against him. The hard planes of his body press against my softer curves, and I have to stifle a gasp. "Shall we find somewhere more... private to continue our discussion?"

Every nerve in my body screams yes, but I force myself to maintain control. I trace a finger along his jaw, feeling the muscle twitch under my touch. "Not yet," I breathe. "I'm not finished with my wine."

Frustration and desire flash in his eyes, quickly

masked by a predatory smile. "Tease," he accuses, but there's no heat in it. He enjoys our game as much as I do.

I take another sip of wine, hyperaware of his gaze on my lips, my throat. "Tell me, Raptor," I say, letting my voice drop to a husky whisper. "What would you do if you had me all to yourself?"

His grip on my hip tightens. "Dangerous question, Silver."

"I like danger."

He chuckles, the sound sending vibrations through me where our bodies touch. "I'd make you beg me to touch you."

The vivid image his words paint makes heat pool low in my belly. "And then?" I prompt, my voice embarrassingly breathy.

Raptor's hand slides lower, toying with the hem of my dress. "Then I'd bite my way up your body and eat you out until you're screaming. I'll fuck you all night long and make your legs shake. You know, like I always do."

I swallow hard, my throat suddenly dry. "You're a little full of yourself."

"I am." His voice is pure sin. "But am I lying?"

"No. You're not." I force myself to step back, instantly missing the heat of his body.

"What are you doing?"

"I can't stay longer tonight. I have other matters that require my attention."

Disappointment and hunger war in his expression before he smooths it into a neutral mask. "You can't run forever, Silver," he warns, his tone a delicious mix of promise and threat.

I lean in, my lips barely brushing his ear. "Who says I'm running?"

With that, I turn and disappear into the crowd, feeling his gaze burning into my back. My heart races, desire and adrenaline singing through my veins. It takes every ounce of willpower I possess not to look back, not to return to his arms and damn the consequences.

But I have work to do.

Back in my apartment, the soft glow of multiple computer screens pushes back the darkness. I slip out of my dress, letting it pool on the floor as I settle into my chair. The juxtaposition of my lace lingerie and the tech surrounding me isn't lost on me—Devin West, society darling and secret hacker, straddling two worlds as always.

I force thoughts of Raptor—of Hawk—aside, focusing on the task at hand. My fingers fly over the keyboard as I slip past firewalls and security protocols, burrowing deep into Regina Black's communications. I press my lips together into a tight line. I've been fighting cyber-attacks on Hawk's business for years. But recently, it's gotten out of control. Someone wants to truly take him down. It's what prompted my return sooner than I planned. Regina's a key player in the dangers to Rivers Financial.

The encrypted messages I intercept paint a troubling picture. Regina's vendetta against Hawk has escalated beyond petty rivalry. She's planning something big —corporate espionage on a scale that could cripple Hawk's latest business venture.

Anger burns hot in my chest. Regina's always been a snake, but this... this is crossing a line. I work methodically, rerouting communications, corrupting key files, planting misinformation that will send Regina's lackeys on wild goose chases.

As I work, a notification pops up on my phone. Another message from Hawk, asking to meet outside of the Den. I hesitate, my finger hovering over the screen. Part of me—a larger part than I care to admit—wants to say yes. To see him in the light of day without the masks and the games.

But that way lies danger. Vulnerability. Loss of control.

I'm about to decline when another thought strikes me. Meeting on my own turf where I have the home-field advantage... that could work to my benefit.

Before I can second-guess myself, I type out a reply.

"*The Sky Bar at the Westbrook Hotel. 8 PM tomorrow. Don't be late.*"

The next evening, I'm nursing a gin and tonic at the bar when Hawk arrives. He cuts an impressive figure in a tailored charcoal suit, and I allow myself a moment to appreciate the view. When his eyes land on me, I see a flash of something—hunger, maybe, or triumph—before his face settles into a polite mask.

"Devin," he says, sliding onto the stool next to me. The sound of my real name on his lips sends a shiver through me. "Thank you for agreeing to meet."

I incline my head, outwardly cool despite the way my heart races. "I was curious about what was so important."

Hawk orders a whiskey neat before turning those piercing eyes on me. "I've been thinking about the night of the gala," he begins, and my body tenses.

"If this is about what happened between us, there's no need to apologize," I interject, my tone sharper than I intended. Panic rises in my throat—is he regretting being with me?

Hawk looks taken aback for a moment. "I just wanted to—"

"We're both adults," I press on, my tone flat,

desperate to regain control of the conversation. "No need for regrets."

The hurt and confusion that flash across Hawk's face make me realize I've miscalculated badly. Embarrassment and anger war within me as I stand abruptly. "I think this was a mistake," I mutter, turning to leave.

I hear Hawk call after me, but I don't stop. I make it to the elevator before he catches up, slipping inside just as the doors are closing.

"What do you want, Hawk?" I demand, staring resolutely at the polished metal doors.

He moves closer, his presence filling the small space. "To clear up this misunderstanding."

I glance up at him, confusion and annoyance warring in my chest. "What misunderstanding?"

"I wanted to apologize for not being conscious when you left," he explains, his voice low and intense. "I wanted to be awake to say good-bye."

His words hit me like a physical blow, and I feel my carefully constructed walls begin to crumble. "Oh," I manage, my voice barely above a whisper.

Hawk reaches out, brushing a strand of hair from my face. The gentle touch sends sparks skittering across my skin. "I don't regret what happened," he says softly. His gentle touch changes the moment his hand wraps around my throat. "Far from it."

My body is instantly ablaze and heat pools between my legs. The hand at my throat squeezes and he pins me against the back of the elevator. I swallow hard, vulnerability threatening to overwhelm me. "Neither do I," I admit, the words come out a hoarse whisper, both a surrender and a victory.

The elevator dings, the doors sliding open to reveal an empty lobby. Neither of us moves. Hawk's gaze drops to my lips, and I know what's coming a split second before it happens.

His kiss is hard, commanding, and all-consuming. Everything I remember and more—passionate, demanding, with an underlying tenderness that makes my knees weak. I return it with equal fervor, months of pent-up desire and longing pouring out in this one perfect moment.

When we finally break apart, I'm breathless and trembling. Hawk's eyes are dark with want, but there's something else there too—a warmth, a connection that goes beyond mere physical attraction.

"Let's get some dinner," he says softly, his thumb tracing my lower lip.

I nod, not trusting myself to speak. As we step out of the elevator, Hawk's hand holds mine, fingers entwined —a gesture both possessive and protective.

I don't feel the need to pull away. Not with Hawk.

I've craved his touch for so long that I'm almost giddy with excitement having him near me. But I can't show it. It would ruin everything.

As we make our way back to the bar, my mind races.

I think of Regina's schemes, of the secrets I'm keeping, and of the delicate balance I've worked so hard to maintain. I know that pursuing this thing with Hawk—whatever it is—will complicate everything and it will give him the upper hand.

But as I feel his fingers squeeze mine while he towers over my side, I realize something.

Some games are worth losing.

And some dangers are worth embracing. And Hawk and I...we have unfinished business.

EIGHT

The city sprawls beneath me, a glittering tapestry of light and shadow. From my office on the top floor of Rivers Tower, I survey my domain with a mixture of pride and simmering rage. The floor-to-ceiling windows offer a panoramic view that never fails to remind me of the power I wield—and the lengths I'll go to maintain it.

I turn from the vista, my attention drawn to the array of screens covering one wall of my office. Each display feeds me real-time data on Rivers Financial's operations, a constant stream of information that I've always found comforting. But lately, that comfort has been eroded by anomalies that I can't explain, and if there's one thing I despise, it's not being in control.

"Hawk, your cybersecurity team is here."

I press a button, for my assistant granting them entry. "Bring them in, Lucas."

The door opens, admitting a group of men and women in crisp suits led by Lucas Grant, my right-hand man. Their faces are a mix of determination and thinly veiled fear. They know the cost of failure in my world.

"Report," I command, settling into my chair behind the imposing mahogany desk. The leather creaks softly, a sound that usually soothes me. Not today.

Lucas steps forward, tablet in hand. His Adam's apple bobs as he swallows hard. "Sir, we've detected a pattern of... assistance. Someone's been intercepting threats to our systems before they can materialize. Financial transactions diverted, security breaches thwarted."

I lean back, fingers steepled, my voice dangerously soft. "And you haven't been able to trace this... benefactor?"

A ripple of discomfort passes through the group. Sweat beads on foreheads, hands clench imperceptibly.

"Not yet," Lucas admits, his voice steady despite the fear in his eyes. "Whoever it is, they're good. Really good."

I feel a muscle twitch in my jaw, the only outward sign of my growing anger. "Not good enough. Find out who's behind this. I want names, motives, everything.

This is private information that's being played with. And if I find out any of you are involved..." I let the threat hang in the air, watching as they pale.

They nod, understanding the implicit promise of violence in my words. As they file out, I call Daniel in. "A moment."

Once we're alone, I fix him with a hard stare. "What aren't you telling me?"

He hesitates, then sighs. "We have a lead. But it's... complicated."

"Spit it out." My patience is wearing thin.

"We believe the interference is coming from Sphinx."

The name hits me like a physical blow. Sphinx—the legendary hacker, untouchable and unidentified for years. I've heard whispers, of course. Everyone in my circles has. But to have Sphinx involved in my affairs...

"Contact them," I order. "Now."

Lucas nods, pulling out his phone to send an encrypted message through channels I prefer not to know about. The response comes back almost immediately, and I can see the frustration on Lucas's face before he even speaks.

"They say only Sphinx can answer our questions, and Sphinx is unavailable to speak at this time."

I feel a surge of anger, my fist slamming down on the

desk. The sound echoes through the office like a gunshot. "They're playing games," I snarl. "But why? What's their angle?"

Lucas flinches but holds his ground. "We don't know, sir. It could be a trap, or they might be after company secrets."

I stand abruptly, pacing behind my desk. If Sphynx wants company secrets, there's nothing I can do about it. Sphynx is the best. Whoever they are, they wouldn't help me to then steal. Something's not adding up. "What do we know about Sphinx's recent activities?"

"Not much, sir. They've been quiet lately. The only notable tech news has been the launch of that new cybersecurity firm, West Securities."

I pause. "Devin West's company?"

Lucas nods. "Yes, sir. They've been making waves in the industry. Devin West herself is said to be highly skilled."

I grunt, recalling the dossier I'd had compiled on Devin when she returned to the city. Her company had caught my attention, but there had been nothing to suggest a connection to Sphinx or any hacker groups.

"Keep digging," I order Lucas. "I want to know everything about West Securities, and I mean everything. But keep it quiet. If Devin West is involved in this, I don't want her tipped off."

As Lucas leaves, I turn back to the window, my mind racing. Why would Sphinx care about Rivers Financial? Are they setting me up? And where does Devin fit into all of this?

The anger builds inside me, a familiar, almost comforting pressure. I need an outlet, and I know just where to find one.

"Daniel," I speak into my secure phone. "Meet me at the warehouse. Bring our... guest."

An hour later, I'm standing in a dimly lit room in an abandoned warehouse on the outskirts of the city. The air is thick with the metallic scent of blood and the acrid stench of fear. In the center of the room, tied to a chair, is the waiter who handed me that drugged champagne at the gala.

His face is already a mess of bruises and cuts from previous "conversations," but I'm far from done with him.

"Who sent you to drug me?" I demand, my voice echoing in the cavernous space.

The waiter spits blood, his eyes defiant. "Go to hell."

I smile, a cold, mirthless expression that makes him shrink back. "Oh, I intend to, but I'm going to send you there first."

My fist connects with his jaw, the satisfying crunch of bone a balm to my frayed nerves. I lose myself in the rhythm of the beating, each blow a release for my pent-up frustration and rage.

I'm dimly aware of Daniel watching from the shadows, his face impassive. He's seen this side of me before, knows when to intervene and when to let me work out my anger.

Time loses meaning. My knuckles are split and bleeding, but I barely feel the pain. The waiter's face is unrecognizable, a swollen mass of torn flesh and shattered bone. His breathing is labored, each inhale a wet, gurgling sound.

"Boss," Daniel's voice cuts through the haze of violence. "That's enough. We still need him alive if we're going to get the name of who asked him to drug you."

I step back, chest heaving, adrenaline coursing through my veins. As the red mist clears from my vision, I realize I've gone too far. The waiter is barely conscious, teetering on the edge of death.

"Clean this up," I order Daniel, my voice hoarse. "Keep him alive. I'm not done with him yet."

As I turn to leave, my bloody hands clenched at my sides, a face flashes in my mind. Devin. Her green eyes, sharp and knowing, seem to pierce through me, judging me for what I've done.

I shake my head, trying to dispel the image. Why am I thinking of her now in this moment of brutality?

Back in my penthouse, I stand under the scalding spray of the shower, watching as the water turns pink with blood—the waiter's and my own. The events of the day swirl in my mind like a toxic whirlpool: Sphinx's interference, Regina's veiled threats, Devin's possible involvement.

As I step out of the shower, wrapping a towel around my waist, I catch sight of my reflection in the steamed-up mirror. My eyes are cold, empty. The face of a man who will do anything to protect what's his.

I press my forehead against the cool glass, closing my eyes for a moment. The weight of my empire presses down on me, a constant reminder of what I stand to lose if I make one wrong move. Like trusting people. I trust only myself.

"Who can I rely on?" I whisper to my reflection.

The thought of reaching out to Devin crosses my mind, but I hesitate. If she is involved in all of this, approaching her directly could tip my hand. And if she's not... well, that presents its own set of complications.

I dress quickly, my mind made up. It's time to take a more active role in this investigation. If Sphinx wants to play games, I'll show them just how dangerous a player I can be.

As the night wears on, I find myself unable to focus. The screens before me blur, the data meaningless in the face of my growing obsession. Devin's face haunts me, her green eyes seeming to mock my efforts to unravel this mystery.

I slam my laptop shut, frustration boiling over. This is ridiculous. I'm Hawk Rivers. I don't get distracted. I don't lose control.

Before I can talk myself out of it, I'm in the elevator, descending to the private garage where my Aston Martin waits. The engine purrs to life, a sound that usually calms me. Tonight, it only fuels my urgency.

The city streaks by in a blur of neon and shadow as I navigate the late-night streets. I know where I'm going, though I've never been there myself. The dossier on Devin included her address—a high-end apartment in a renovated industrial building. The kind of place that values privacy and discretion.

I park a block away, my heart pounding with an unfamiliar rhythm. Is it anticipation? Fear? I'm not used to this uncertainty, and I don't like it.

The lobby is deserted at this hour, the night concierge barely glancing up as I stride past. The elevator ride to her floor feels interminable. With each passing second, I question my decision to come here. I can't stay away from her. Every second feels like a fucking eternity and I'm not sure

But it's too late to turn back now. I'm standing in front of her door, my hand raised to knock. For a moment, I hesitate.

I knock, three sharp raps that echo in the quiet hallway.

Seconds stretch into eternity. I'm about to turn away, cursing myself for this moment of weakness, when I hear movement inside. The soft padding of bare feet on hardwood. A pause.

The door opens, and there she is. Devin, dressed in silk pajamas, her dark hair tousled as if she'd been tossing and turning in bed. She's fucking perfect. The anger and frustration from the day disappear as I stare at her. Her eyes widen in surprise, then narrow with something that might be suspicion… or interest.

"Hawk." My name sounds so fucking good coming out of her mouth. "What are you doing here?"

Devin studies me for a long moment, her gaze so penetrating I feel exposed in a way I never have before. Then, without a word, she steps back, opening the door wider.

And even if I don't want to admit it, she's in control tonight.

NINE

The city pulses around me, a living, breathing entity of concrete and steel. But tonight, its familiar rhythm feels off, discordant. Something's wrong. I can feel it in the air, in the way the shadows seem to lengthen and reach for me as I approach my apartment building.

The lobby is deserted, the usual security guard conspicuously absent. My heart rate quickens, instincts honed by years of living on the edge screaming danger. I take the stairs instead of the elevator, my footsteps silent on the concrete steps.

Five floors up, I reach my door and freeze. It's ajar, the frame splintered around the lock. Ice floods my veins, but my mind remains crystal clear. They've found me. Not as Sphinx—that identity is still secure—but as a suspected member of the Hacker Alliance. Viktor Kazanov, in his paranoid fury, is casting a wide net. Bastard. He just can't handle that I was able to dismantle a leg of his organization without even trying.

I push the door open, wincing at the soft creak. The sight that greets me turns my stomach, even as my face remains impassive. My sanctuary, my carefully ordered world, lies in ruins. Furniture overturned, glass shattered, and my precious tech—my lifeline—reduced to sparking, broken husks.

"Amateurs," I mutter, eyes scanning for any remaining threats. The destruction is thorough but sloppy. They were looking for something specific—probably proof of my connection to the Alliance—but they clearly don't know what they're dealing with.

No time to mourn the loss. I move swiftly, gathering essentials. A concealed laptop, untouched by the destruction. Encrypted flash drives. A stash of cash and passports hidden behind a loose baseboard. My fingers brush cool metal, and I pull out a compact firearm, checking the magazine with practiced efficiency.

There's one more thing, the most dangerous of all. I pry up a floorboard, revealing a small black box. Inside lies enough information to bring Viktor's entire operation crashing down. It's my insurance policy, my leverage. And now, possibly, my death sentence.

A creak outside the door sends adrenaline surging through me. I glance at my smartwatch, a custom piece that links to the building's security feeds. Multiple unidentified figures, converging on my location.

"Showtime," I whisper, a grim smile playing on my lips. I may be outnumbered, but I'm far from outmatched.

As I step into the hallway, four men block my path, their expressions cold and predatory. I recognize the look in their eyes—the dead-eyed stare of men who kill without remorse.

"Going somewhere?" one sneers, his jacket shifting to reveal the gleam of a weapon.

I assess my options in a heartbeat. Four against one. Narrow hallway. Emergency exit at the far end, if I can reach it. My mind calculates trajectories, angles, weak points.

"Boys," I say, my voice dripping with false sweetness, "I don't suppose you'd believe I ordered a pizza?"

They don't waste time on banter. The first one lunges, all brute force and no finesse. I sidestep, using his momentum to send him crashing into the wall. His head connects with a sickening crack, and he crumples.

The second comes at me with a knife, the blade whistling through the air. I duck under his swing, grabbing his wrist and twisting sharply. The knife clatters to the floor as he howls in pain. A quick jab to his solar plexus, and he's down, gasping for air.

"Come on," I taunt the remaining two, falling into a fighting stance. "I thought Viktor only hired the best."

They attack in tandem, trying to overwhelm me with sheer numbers. But I'm in my element now, my body moving on pure instinct and years of training. I weave and dodge, my fists and feet finding vulnerable points with surgical precision. Ribs crack, joints dislocate, and bodies hit the floor.

For a moment, I allow myself a flicker of satisfaction. Four highly trained killers, neutralized in under a minute. Not bad for a night's work.

But then more appear from the stairwell, and suddenly the odds shift dramatically. I'm good, but even I have limits. A heavy blow catches me in the side, and I stagger, gasping for breath.

Rough hands grab me, twisting my arm behind my back. Another goon moves to restrain my legs. For a moment, real fear grips me. This is it. This is how I die, in a dingy hallway at the hands of faceless thugs.

And then, like an avenging angel straight out of hell, Hawk appears.

"How dare you touch my woman," he snarls, his voice colder than I've ever heard it. The words send a jolt through me—equal parts shock, indignation, and...

something else. Something I'm not ready to examine too closely.

But there's no time to dwell on it. Hawk moves like a force of nature, all coiled power and lethal precision. I watch in awe as he systematically dismantles my attackers, each blow calculated for maximum damage. Bones crack, bodies crumple, and all the while, Hawk's expression remains chillingly calm.

One man pulls a gun, but Hawk is faster. He grabs the thug's wrist, twisting until the bones snap audibly. The gun falls, and Hawk catches it midair, putting a bullet between the man's eyes without hesitation.

His brutality should horrify me. Instead, I feel a dark thrill. This is Hawk unleashed, raw and primal. And God help me, it's intoxicating.

I snap out of my daze, using the distraction to break free from my captors. Hawk and I fall into sync without a word, covering each other's blind spots, our movements a deadly dance. It feels right in a way I can't explain, as if we've been fighting side by side our whole lives.

"Behind you!" I shout, dropping low as Hawk spins, his elbow connecting with an attacker's throat. The man goes down, clutching his crushed windpipe.

I sweep the legs out from under another, following

through with a brutal stomp to his knee. The crack of bone is oddly satisfying.

When it's over, the hallway is littered with groaning, unconscious bodies—and a few that will never move again. Hawk turns to me, concern flickering in his steel-gray eyes. "Are you hurt?"

I wipe blood from my split lip, suddenly aware of the various aches blossoming across my body. "Nothing I can't handle," I reply, aiming for nonchalance. "Though I had it under control before you crashed the party."

Hawk's lips twitch in what might be amusement. "Of course, you did. But they touched what's mine. That demands a response."

Irritation flares, warring with the part of me that wants to collapse into his arms. "I'm not yours," I snap, even as a traitorous part of me thrills at the possessiveness in his voice.

"Aren't you?" Hawk steps closer, his eyes burning with an intensity that steals my breath. "You're coming with me. It's not safe here."

I want to argue, to assert my independence. But the rational part of my brain knows he's right. I'm in over my head, and my sanctuary is compromised. "Fine," I concede, hating how small my voice sounds. "But this doesn't change anything. I don't need a protector."

Hawk's expression softens fractionally. "Maybe not. But even the strongest warriors need allies, Devin."

The sincerity in his voice catches me off guard. For a moment, I allow myself to imagine it—Hawk and I, a united front against the world. It's a seductive thought, and all the more dangerous for it.

As we leave, I notice the discreet arrival of unmarked vehicles. Hawk's people, no doubt, here to clean up the mess. It's a stark reminder of the power he wields and the resources at his disposal. And now, it seems, all of that is being mobilized to protect me.

The thought is both comforting and terrifying.

Hawk guides me to his car, a sleek, armored beast that practically screams wealth and danger. As we pull away from the curb, I stare out at the city lights, my mind a whirlwind of conflicting thoughts.

"Viktor's men," Hawk starts, "don't usually come in such numbers." He spares me a quick dark glance. "What did they want?"

"They are interested in my connection to the Hacker Alliance."

His head snaps sideways and pins me with his gaze. "You're a part?"

I stare right back. "I am."

"So you know Sphinx?"

I laugh. "The Alliance is large. Only a handful of

very privileged people know Sphinx. What makes you think I do?"

His gaze focuses on the road again. "I didn't know you were part of the Alliance."

I shrug. "Was I supposed to tell you?"

We reach his building and he parks the car and turns to me, one hand going to my throat and making me wet. "I know everything about you, Devin." He leans into me, his face inches from mine. "But I didn't know that." The hand around my throat squeezes and my eyes close instinctively. He squeezes harder. "I don't like surprises."

I pull at his hand but his fingers are a vice around my throat. "It's not my fault you have idiots working for you," I choke out.

His hand moves to the back of my neck and yanks me forward, our lips clashing in a rough kiss. The kiss is a brand, a reminder that I belong to him. But I kiss him back just as hard, just as rough, and take it a step further and bite him. *You're mine, Hawk.* We're both breathing heavily when we part and neither willing to back down.

Hawk's knuckles whiten on the steering wheel. "I'll deal with Viktor," he says, his tone promising violence.

"No," I say sharply. "I can handle Viktor."

Hawk glances at me, his expression unreadable.

"You don't have to do everything alone, Devin. Not anymore."

His words stir something in me, a longing I've kept buried for years. But I can't afford to give in to it. Not now, not with so much at stake.

"We'll see," I murmur.

He saved me tonight, but at what cost? The balance of power between us has shifted, and I'm not sure I like which way the scales are tipping.

TEN

The city sprawls beneath my office window, a chessboard of power and opportunity. But for once, my mind isn't on business deals or hostile takeovers. It's consumed by thoughts of Devin—her fierce green eyes, the curve of her neck, the way she fits perfectly in my arms. My woman. The words echo in my mind, a possessive mantra that sets my blood on fire.

A soft knock interrupts my brooding. "Come in," I growl, not bothering to turn around.

"Still brooding by windows, I see. Some things never change."

My sister Olivia's voice snaps me back to the present. I turn, forcing a smile that doesn't quite reach my eyes. "Welcome home, Liv."

We exchange pleasantries, but my mind is elsewhere. I need information, and Olivia is my best source.

"Tell me everything about Devin," I demand, cutting through the small talk. "Every detail, no matter how small that you may not have shared while you were abroad."

Olivia raises an eyebrow at my tone. "She's fine, Hawk. Safe and sound, thanks to you."

"That's not enough," I snap, pacing the room like a caged animal. "Kazanov is still out there. He dared to touch what's mine. I want him erased from existence."

"Hawk," Olivia warns, but I cut her off with a look that would make most men tremble.

"No one threatens Devin. No one." My voice is low, dangerous. "I'll burn this entire city to the ground if that's what it takes to keep her safe."

Olivia studies me for a long moment. "You really love her, don't you?"

The question catches me off guard. Love? Is that what this all-consuming need is? This desire to possess Devin completely, to keep her safe from the world and claim her as my own?

"She's mine," I say simply as if that explains everything. And in my mind, it does.

"Did she... was there anyone else?" The question

burns in my throat, jealousy clawing at my insides. "While you were away, did she..."

Olivia's expression softens. "No one, Hawk. A few guys tried to be friends, but—"

"Names," I interrupt, my voice like ice. "I want names."

"Hawk, you can't be serious—"

"Names, Olivia." My tone leaves no room for argument.

She sighs, recognizing the futility of resisting. As she lists off a few meaningless names, I make mental notes. These men dared to think they could have a claim on Devin. They need to be... dealt with.

"—but you were the only man she ever really talked about," Olivia finishes, eyeing me warily.

Satisfaction blooms in my chest, dark and possessive. "Good," I murmur, already planning how to eliminate any potential rivals.

"Now, about Kazanov," Olivia says, clearly trying to steer the conversation to safer ground. "What exactly happened?"

The reminder of Kazanov's attack reignites my rage. In my mind's eye, I see Devin surrounded by his thugs, and something inside me snaps.

"He sent men to her apartment," I snarl, my fist connecting with the wall hard enough to crack the plaster. "They put their filthy hands on her. They tried to take her from me."

Olivia flinches at the display of violence, but I'm beyond caring. "I'll destroy him," I continue, my voice eerily calm despite the storm raging inside me. "I'll dismantle his entire operation piece by piece. And then, when he has nothing left, I'll make him watch as I take everything he values before I end his miserable existence."

"Hawk," Olivia says softly, reaching out to touch my arm. I jerk away, not wanting to be soothed. "We need to be smart about this. Rushing in could put Devin in more danger."

Her words penetrate the haze of my anger. Devin. Everything comes back to keeping her safe. Keeping her mine.

"Fine," I concede, reining in my rage with considerable effort. "We'll do this your way. For now. But make no mistake, Olivia. Kazanov is a dead man walking. It's just a matter of time."

Olivia nods, relief evident in her eyes. "I'll keep digging, see what I can find out about Devin's connection to Kazanov. You focus on keeping her safe—without smothering her. You know how she values her independence."

I scoff at the idea. Independence. As if Devin could

ever truly be separate from me now. We're entwined, our fates interlinked. She just doesn't want to accept it.

"I'll protect her," I say, my tone leaving no doubt as to the lengths I'll go. "Whatever it takes."

As Olivia prepares to leave, a thought occurs to me. "Liv," I call, stopping her at the door. "Don't tell Devin about this conversation. About any of it. She doesn't need to know... the depths of my concern."

Olivia gives me a long, searching look. "All right," she says finally. "But Hawk, be careful. This obsession... it's not healthy."

I smile, and there's nothing warm in it. "Health is overrated, little sister. Power is what matters. And I have enough power to keep Devin safe with me. Forever."

As the door closes behind Olivia, I turn back to the window. The city lies before me, full of threats to eliminate and obstacles to overcome. But none of it matters. Only Devin matters.

My Devin. Mine to protect. Mine to possess.

Mine to love in my own dark, all-consuming way.

Let Kazanov come. Let the whole world try to take her from me. They'll learn the hard way what happens when someone touches what belongs to Hawk Rivers.

THE SLEEK, modern office around me hums with quiet efficiency, but my mind is a storm of plots and calculations. I glance at the two burly security guards positioned discreetly by the door, their dark suits and earpieces a stark reminder of Hawk's overprotectiveness. I'd argued vehemently against them, but Hawk's steely gaze had made it clear: no guards, no leaving the penthouse.

"Compromise," he'd called it, his voice a low growl that sent shivers down my spine. I call it a tactical retreat—for now.

My fingers fly over the keyboard, lines of code scrolling past as I devise new ways to dismantle Kazanov's empire, bit by digital bit. The soft blue glow of the monitors casts shadows across my face, reflecting in my eyes like glacial ice. But Kazanov's not my only target.

Regina's smug face flashes in my mind, her perfectly manicured hand on Hawk's arm at the banquet. My jaw clenches involuntarily, teeth grinding. She touched what's mine. She'll pay for that.

A notification pops up on my screen—a message from Max, my assistant and one of the few Hacker Alliance employees who knows my true identity.

Max: Got those financials you wanted on Black

Industries. Looks like Regina's been cooking the books. Sending details now.

A predatory smile curves my lips, sharp enough to cut. "Perfect," I murmur, already envisioning Regina's downfall.

A soft knock interrupts my plotting. I look up to see Olivia standing in the doorway, a vision of elegance in a cream silk blouse and tailored trousers. My best friend, Hawk's sister, and the one person who's been by my side through it all.

"Liv!" I exclaim, genuinely happy to see her. The ice in my veins thaws, just a little. "When did you get back?"

She crosses the room, enveloping me in a warm hug that smells of jasmine and home. "Just yesterday. Figured I'd let you settle in before ambushing you." Her eyes twinkle mischievously. "Lunch?"

Twenty minutes later, we're ensconced in a private booth at Le Petit Jardin, an upscale restaurant that caters to those who value discretion. Crystal chandeliers cast a soft glow over the crisp white tablecloths, and the gentle murmur of conversation provides a soothing backdrop. As we peruse the menu, Olivia's gaze turns speculative over the rim of her water glass.

"So," she begins casually, setting down her glass with a soft clink, "you and my brother…"

I take a sip of water, buying time. "What about us?"

Olivia raises an eyebrow, her expression a mix of amusement and concern. "Come on, Dev. I leave you two alone for a few months, and suddenly you're living in his penthouse?"

"Temporarily," I clarify, a hint of defensiveness creeping into my voice. "It's just until this situation with Kazanov blows over."

"Mm-hmm," Olivia hums, clearly unconvinced. "And how's that going? Being back in Hawk's orbit?"

I allow myself a small smile, memories of heated encounters flashing through my mind—Hawk's burning gaze, his possessive touch, the way he says my name like a prayer and a curse all at once. "It's... intense. But I've got it under control. It's on my terms."

Olivia's expression turns serious, her fork pausing halfway to her mouth. "Dev, you know I love you, but... Hawk isn't someone anyone can control. He's dangerous when he wants something."

A thrill runs through me at her words, but I keep my face neutral. "I know exactly who your brother is, Liv. And what I'm doing."

What I don't say is how much I crave that danger, that intensity. How the thought of Hawk's possessive gaze makes my skin tingle with anticipation. How I lie awake at night, plotting ways to draw him in closer while maintaining my independence. It's a delicate dance, a game of power and control that sets my blood on fire.

But Olivia doesn't need to know that. For all our years of friendship, there are parts of me I keep hidden even from her. The obsessive thoughts, the dark desires, the ruthless ambition that mirrors Hawk's own—these are mine alone.

"If you say so," Olivia concedes, though concern still lingers in her eyes. "Just... be careful, okay?"

I reach across the table, squeezing her hand. "Always am. And Liv? Thank you. For everything you've done for me. I wouldn't be who I am without you."

Olivia's face softens, and she laughs, the sound light and carefree. "Oh, please. As if you needed any help becoming a force of nature." Her eyes take on a mischievous glint. "Remember college? All those guys falling over themselves to ask you out?"

I groan, but there's no real annoyance behind it. "Don't remind me. What was that one guy's name? The one who showed up at our dorm with a full mariachi band?"

"Trevor!" Olivia exclaims, nearly choking on her wine. "I thought you were going to murder him on the spot."

"I considered it," I admit, a wry smile tugging at my lips. "But that would have been messy. And loud."

Olivia shakes her head, still chuckling. "You know, it's funny. All those guys, and you never gave any of them a second glance. Not after..."

"Not after what?" I prompt, though I know exactly what she's referring to.

"Your 18th birthday party," Olivia says softly.

I feel heat creep up my neck, but I force myself to maintain eye contact. "I don't know what you're talking about," I lie smoothly.

Olivia just smiles, knowing and a little sad. "Of course, you don't."

For a moment, I'm tempted to tell her everything. About the secret Hawk and I share, the one known only to us and my parents. But I hold my tongue. Some secrets are too precious, too dangerous to voice aloud.

The moment is interrupted by my phone buzzing insistently. Max's name flashes on the screen.

"I have to take this," I say, already slipping into business mode. "Max? What have you got for me?"

As Max relays the information, a plan crystallizes in my mind. My expression hardens, a cold determination settling over me like a second skin. "Do it," I order, my voice leaving no room for argument. "Liquidate their assets, all of them. I want Kazanov's shell companies gutted by morning."

I end the call, looking up to find Olivia staring at me with wide eyes. For a moment, I wonder if I've revealed too much of my true nature.

But then Olivia's lips quirk into a wry smile. "You know," she says slowly, swirling the wine in her glass, "I think I might have underestimated just how perfectly matched you and my brother really are."

I allow myself a genuine laugh, the tension dissipating. I raise my glass in a mock toast, "You have no idea."

As we return to our meal, my mind is already racing ahead, plotting my next moves. Kazanov, Regina, even Hawk—they're all pieces on my chessboard. And I intend to win this game, no matter the cost.

Let them underestimate me. Let them think they have the upper hand. I'll show them all exactly who Devin West really is—and God help anyone who stands in my way.

The secret Hawk and I share pulses between us, unspoken but ever-present. And it's the key to everything.

ELEVEN

The city sprawls beneath me, a glittering tapestry of light and shadow. From Hawk's penthouse, I should feel on top of the world. Instead, I'm burning from the inside out, trapped in a gilded cage of luxury and desire.

My fingers twitch, itching for control. Hawk's "protection" may confine me physically, but in the digital realm, I'm still Sphinx—untouchable, unstoppable.

I retrieve my custom-built hacking tool, disguised as a sleek smartphone. To the casual observer, I'm just another socialite. If only they knew the chaos I'm about to unleash.

Bypassing Hawk's state-of-the-art security is child's play. I slip into his network like a ghost leaving no trace.

From there, Viktor Kazanov's systems beckon, a siren call I can't resist.

"Let's see what secrets you're hiding, Viktor," I murmur, diving into the depths of his digital empire.

Layer after layer of cybersecurity falls before me. It's intoxicating, this power. In here, I'm not Devin West, the heiress under house arrest. I'm the shadow that haunts Viktor's nightmares.

I locate his personal cell phone data, tapping into a real-time feed of his calls and messages. Viktor's voice fills my ears, cold and calculated.

"Lay low until I give the signal," he commands his lieutenants. "We need to identify who is sabotaging our operations before we deal with Devin West."

My heart races. He knows. Not everything, but enough to be on guard.

"There's a possibility she's connected to the Hacker Alliance," Viktor continues. "Maybe even Sphinx."

A smirk tugs at my lips. "So close, yet so far," I think, adrenaline coursing through my veins.

Time to remind Viktor why he should fear the shadows.

I dive deeper, planting false information like toxic seeds. Financial records scramble, shipments reroute to nonexistent destinations, fabricated messages sow discord among his top lieutenants. A virus, elegant in its simplicity, begins to eat away at his data.

The sound of the penthouse door opening snaps me back to reality. I secure my device in an instant, my pulse quickening as Hawk strides in, a predator in a perfectly tailored suit.

Our eyes lock. The air crackles, charged with unspoken hunger.

"You're back early," I say, aiming for nonchalance but hearing the breathless quality in my voice.

Hawk's gaze rakes over me, hot enough to burn. "Miss me?" The corner of his mouth quirks up, knowing and dangerous.

"You wish," I retort, but we both hear the lie.

He moves closer, each step deliberate. I force myself to stand my ground, even as every nerve-ending screams for contact.

"You can't keep me here forever," I say, needing to push back, to feel some semblance of control.

Hawk chuckles, the sound vibrating through me. "Can't I?" He's close now, close enough that I can smell his cologne. "Face it, Devin. You don't want to leave."

His words hit too close to home. I turn away, needing distance, but he catches my wrist. His touch sends electricity arcing through my body.

"Let go," I demand, but there's no real fight in it.

"Make me," Hawk challenges, voice low and rough.

I spin back to face him, ready to argue, but the words die in my throat. His eyes are storm-gray, pupils blown wide with desire. For me.

"This game," Hawk murmurs, pulling me closer until we're chest to chest, "is dangerous."

"I like danger," I breathe, tilting my chin up defiantly.

A growl rumbles through Hawk's chest. "Careful what you wish for, little mouse."

His free hand comes up to cup my face, thumb brushing over my lower lip. I can't help the small gasp that escapes me, and Hawk's eyes darken further.

"What do you really want, Devin?" he asks, his voice barely above a whisper.

The truth claws its way up my throat, impossible to deny. "You," I admit. "I want you."

Triumph flashes in Hawk's eyes. "That's my girl," he says before crushing his mouth to mine.

The kiss is all-consuming, a clash of teeth and tongues. I moan into it, fingers curling into the lapels of his jacket. Hawk's hand slides into my hair, gripping tightly, angling my head for deeper access.

When we finally break apart, we're both panting. Hawk's usually immaculate hair is mussed where I've run my fingers through it. The sight sends a thrill of satisfaction through me.

"You're playing with fire," Hawk warns, but there's a note of admiration in his voice.

I smirk, feeling bold. "Maybe I want to get burned."

Hawk's eyes flash dangerously. In one fluid motion, he has me pinned against the wall, his body a solid wall of heat against mine. "Be careful what you ask for, sweetheart," he growls. "I might not be so gentle next time."

The threat—or is it a promise?—sends a shiver of anticipation down my spine. "Who says I want gentle?"

Hawk's laugh is dark and full of promise. "Oh, Devin," he murmurs, lips brushing against my ear. "The things I'm going to do to you..."

I arch against him, craving more contact. But a small part of my brain, the part not consumed by desire, reminds me of the danger we're in. Of Viktor's words, of the looming threat.

"Wait," I gasp, pushing against Hawk's chest. "There's something you need to know."

Hawk pulls back slightly, concern mingling with the lust in his eyes. "What is it?"

I take a deep breath, steeling myself. "Viktor. He's planning something. I... I overheard a conversation."

Hawk's expression hardens, the predator returning. "Tell me everything."

As I recount Viktor's words, leaving out the details of how I obtained this information, I watch Hawk's mind shift into strategic mode. It's mesmerizing, seeing him switch from lover to commander in an instant.

"We'll handle Viktor," Hawk says once I've finished, his tone leaving no room for argument. "Together."

The word sends a thrill through me. Together. It's dangerous, this connection between us. But God help me, I crave it.

Before I can respond, he's kissing me again, softer this time but no less intense. When we part, I'm breathless.

"Now," Hawk says, a wicked glint in his eye, "where were we?"

TWELVE

As we stumble toward the bedroom, hands grasping, lips seeking, I know I'm lost. Viktor, the danger, the outside world—none of it matters. There's only Hawk, only this all-consuming need.

Our clothes came off and he eats me up with a possessive glance. I want Hawk so badly. He's my drug and I can't stay away.

"Come here," he commands. I am not in the mood to let him be in charge. At least, not yet.

"No."

I go against my word and step forward. My pent-up need begs for release. It's always like this with him. I brush my lips over his chest, flicking my tongue over his nipple. He groans and it's enough to make my knees shake. The sound he makes is worth everything.

He slides a hand into my hair, gripping a bunch from the root and holding me in place. I don't care that it hurts. I don't care if tears gather in my eyes. All I care about is Hawk's pleasure right now.

The way he takes short breaths and holds himself tense speaks volumes about his tight rein on his control. He's fighting a losing battle. I want to tell him to let go, but it'll only make him fight even more.

I kiss my way down his body until I'm kneeling before him, his cock standing proud in front of me. I want to worship him with my body. My man. I want to lick and bite him and leave my mark all over him. I lick my lips and glance up at him, all the while stroking his length with my hand.

"You on your knees is a beautiful sight," he says. He looks so turned-on. The fact I can have this effect on him isn't lost on me. Having seen his reaction to other women wanting his attention but only I can get him to lose control is absolutely empowering.

"I bet I can look even better."

He watches me with a dark and dangerous glint in his eyes. "My cock in your hand does look good."

I grin. "Oh, I can do better than that." I lean forward

and circle my tongue over his length. He sucks in a sharp breath.

"Fucking hell, Devin. You love games, don't you?"

I do. I fucking love every second of our game.

"I can't wait to be inside your tight, wet pussy," his voice is rough and low. So sexy. I don't know how he can get these reactions from my body. I am instantly ready to orgasm just from the mental image of what he said.

I slide him out of my mouth and meet his gaze as I glide my tongue over his length before gliding him down my throat.

"I want my cum all over your body."

I do too. I want him to do whatever he wants with me, as long as it's him, I don't care.

"Look at me."

I glance up and meet his gaze. He thrusts deep down my throat until I almost choke. I grip his ass cheeks, taking all of him into my mouth. Tears roll down my cheeks and I gag but I love how he grips my hair.

"I. Can't. Fucking. Wait."

His words are broken and I become fascinated with the need to have him come down my throat. I jerk and suck hard, tight, until my jaw aches, and swear I won't be able to speak or chew for a week. But I don't care. I just want him filling my mouth with his cum.

He tenses and thrusts hard one more time into my

mouth. I make so many gagging noises and he finally loses it. He comes gripping my hair and shooting his cum down my throat. When I finish swallowing, he helps me up to my feet and kisses me. The kiss is hot, greedy, and he immediately shoves a hand between my legs. "So fucking wet. I can't wait to devour you."

Neither can I. "Then do it. Eat me. Fuck me. Make me come."

I sit on the bed and spread my legs wide for him. He kneels and pulls me to the edge, draping my legs over his shoulders.

He kisses my inner thigh and grins. It's full of promise and danger. Then he licks a spiral over my clit and I see stars. "You taste fucking delicious."

My pussy's slick and I want to come. It's hard for me to breathe when my entire focus is on falling off this cliff that Hawk is dangling me over.

"Hawk…"

"Say my name like that again," he orders.

"Hawk, please," I finally give in and beg.

He swipes his tongue over my clit and then thrusts into me, licking and sucking. I gulp, wiggling in his grasp. I'm so close. He sucks harder. I jerk and scream. My orgasm tears through me like a storm over tornado alley. Quick and devastating.

I don't have a chance to catch my breath before he's

on me, instantly driving deep into my still-quivering sex. He kisses me and immediately takes control. Every thrust is a branding. He owns me. I moan and beg again.

I've never felt a hunger, no, a need like this before. I am desperate for him. I want to be his forever. To be taken, owned, and kept by him.

His thrusts are deep and fast, keeping me lost in the sea of need. Pressure builds so fast, I gasp when he grinds deep into me. The dam inside me breaks. My body shakes as a tide of pleasure swallows me. I curl my body into him, holding him hostage while I ride the storm. The lines of his face tighten and he holds himself rigid above me.

"Fuck!"

Yes. Finally. He groans and his rigidity melts from his frame as he fills me with his cum. We pant in unison, both trying to catch our breaths. I caress his back and smile. I love this man.

THIRTEEN

The satisfying crunch of bone beneath my fist reverberates through the gym. My sparring partner crumples, gasping for air. I step back, chest heaving, adrenaline coursing through my veins. It's not enough. The burn in my muscles, the sting of split knuckles—it's all just white noise compared to the thoughts churning in my mind.

Devin.

Her name echoes in my head like a siren's call, equal parts temptation and warning. I grab a towel, wiping sweat from my brow as I move to the tablet perched on a nearby bench. Security reports flicker to life, a digital mosaic of Viktor Kazanov's crumbling empire. Cyber-attacks, misinformation campaigns, financial discrepancies—all executed with surgical precision.

A smirk tugs at my lips. It's her handiwork, no doubt. The realization sends a jolt of electricity down my spine, arousal mingling with a hint of danger. Devin's not just a pretty face with a sharp mind—she's a force of nature, capable of toppling empires from behind a screen.

I close my eyes, inhaling deeply. The scent of sweat and leather fills my nostrils, grounding me. When I open them again, my reflection stares back from the mirrored wall. The man I see is hungry, not just for power or control, but for her.

Hours later, I step into the penthouse, the scent of garlic and wine greeting me. Devin stands at the stove, her back to me. For a moment, I allow myself to drink in the sight of her—the curve of her hips, the elegant line of her neck. She turns, a small smile playing on those tempting lips.

"Perfect timing," she says, lifting a bottle of wine. "Care to do the honors?"

I cross the room in measured strides, taking the bottle from her hands. Our fingers brush, and I feel her pulse quicken. She's good at hiding it, but I catch the almost imperceptible hitch in her breath. I lean in close, my lips a whisper away from her ear.

"My pleasure," I murmur, enjoying the slight shiver that runs through her.

We settle at the dining table, the city sprawling below us like a glittering carpet. Devin takes a sip of wine, her tongue darting out to catch a stray drop on her lower lip. My eyes track the movement, heat coiling in my gut.

"When do you think it'll be safe for me to return to my apartment?" she asks, her tone deceptively casual.

I study her over the rim of my glass, noting the way her fingers tighten almost imperceptibly around the stem. The diamonds around the emerald stone on her ring sparkle in the low light. "You're eager to leave?"

"I appreciate your hospitality," she says, meeting my gaze. "But I miss my own space. Besides, it seems Viktor has backed off."

"What makes you think Viktor has stopped pursuing you?" I press, leaning forward slightly.

Devin pauses, and I can almost see the gears turning behind those captivating eyes. "Just a feeling," she answers after a moment. "Things have been quiet lately."

"A feeling?" I echo, my voice low and charged. "Or do you know something I don't?"

She shrugs, the movement graceful and practiced. "I've been keeping my ears open. Word on the street is that Viktor has bigger problems."

"Interesting," I remark, standing slowly. I move

behind her chair, my hands coming to rest on her shoulders. I feel her tense slightly under my touch. "Considering how closely I monitor such matters, it's curious that you're better informed."

Devin tilts her head back, looking up at me. There's a challenge in her eyes that makes my blood sing. "Perhaps you underestimate my connections."

I lean down, my lips brushing against the shell of her ear. "Maybe it's time you tell me more about these connections," I suggest, my voice a low growl.

She stands abruptly, moving toward the window. I follow, drawn to her like a shark to blood in the water. "You can't control everything," she says softly, looking out over the city.

I press against her back, caging her between my body and the glass. "Control keeps people alive in our world," I respond, my hands settling on her hips. "I can't protect you if I don't know the whole story."

"Maybe I don't need protecting," she whispers, but I feel the way she leans into me, contradicting her words.

Later as moonlight paints shadows across our tangled bodies, Devin's voice breaks the silence. "Do you ever feel trapped?"

I turn to look at her, struck by the vulnerability in her tone. It's a crack in her armor, one I'm all too eager to exploit. "What do you mean?"

"Like no matter where you go, you're confined by expectations, by the walls you've built," she explains, her gaze fixed on the ceiling.

I reach out, tracing the line of her jaw with my fingertips. "I know that feeling all too well," I admit, the honesty surprising even me. "Control can become its own kind of prison."

Devin sighs, the sound heavy with unspoken burdens. "Sometimes I wonder if it's worth it—the secrets, the constant vigilance."

I pull her closer, relishing the feel of her skin against mine. "We all wear masks to protect ourselves," I say softly. "But maybe it's time to let someone in."

She looks at me, conflict swirling in the depths of her eyes. "Easier said than done," she replies, her voice barely above a whisper.

"Perhaps we can start by being honest with each other," I suggest, my tone sincere. It's a calculated risk, this offer of vulnerability. But I know Devin well enough by now to see the lie in her eager nod, the insincerity in her quick agreement.

"No more half-truths," I propose, watching her face carefully. "No more evasion."

"Agreed," she concedes, but I catch the slight tightening around her eyes, the almost imperceptible tension in her jaw. She's lying, and we both know it.

As we settle back into bed, a supposed new understanding between us, I find myself analyzing every word, every gesture. Devin thinks she's won this round, that she's placated me with promises of honesty. But I've spent a lifetime reading people, deciphering the language of body and breath. She's an open book to me, every page screaming of secrets yet untold.

I pull her closer, my hand splaying possessively across her stomach. She melts into me, her body betraying what her words won't. This push and pull between us, this dance of truth and lies—it's intoxicating. Dangerous. Addictive.

"I've been used to handling things alone," I murmur against her skin, feeling her shiver in response. "It's not easy for me to rely on others."

"You're not the only one," Devin responds softly, her fingers intertwining with mine. "Maybe we can learn together."

I smile in the darkness, knowing she can't see the predatory edge to it. "I'd like that," I say, sealing the words with a kiss that's equal parts promise and threat.

FOURTEEN

The sleek black car glides to a stop in front of the West family estate. I take a deep breath, steeling myself for the evening ahead. Hawk's hand finds mine, a gentle squeeze offering silent support. His touch grounds me, a reminder that I'm not the same vulnerable girl I once was.

"Ready?" Hawk asks, his gray eyes searching mine.

I nod, allowing a small smile to curve my lips. "As I'll ever be."

We step out into the cool evening air, the grand mansion looming before us. Crystal chandeliers sparkle through towering windows, casting a warm glow on the immaculately manicured lawns. The soft strains of a string quartet drift across the grounds, mingling with the low hum of conversation and the clink of champagne flutes.

Hawk offers his arm, and I take it, my fingers curling around the crisp fabric of his tuxedo. As we ascend the marble steps, I scan the crowd for a familiar face. My heart lightens when I spot Olivia, her honey-blonde waves unmistakable even from a distance.

"I see Olivia," I murmur to Hawk. "I should go say hello."

He nods, a hint of warmth softening his usually stoic expression. "Of course. I'll find you later."

I make my way through the throng of guests, many of whom turn to whisper as I pass. The weight of their stares prickles at my skin, but I keep my chin high refusing to show any sign of discomfort.

"Devin!" Olivia's warm voice cuts through the noise, and suddenly she's there, wrapping me in a tight embrace. "I'm so glad you're here. How are you holding up?"

I return the hug, allowing myself a moment of genuine comfort in my best friend's arms. "I'm managing," I reply softly, pulling back to meet her concerned gaze. "Thanks for checking in on me the other day. Lunch was... a much-needed break."

Olivia's eyes, so similar to her brother's, search my face. "Of course. That's what best friends are for, right?"

She lowers her voice, glancing around to ensure we're not overheard. "Have you told Hawk about..."

I shake my head minutely. "Not yet. It's... complicated."

She sighs, squeezing my hand. "I know. But Devin, he's worried about you. We both are."

Before I can respond, a familiar voice sends ice through my veins. "Devin, darling, it's been too long."

I turn to face Regina, forcing a polite smile. "Regina. Always a pleasure."

Her eyes flick to where Hawk stands across the room deep in conversation with a group of businessmen. "I see you've brought quite the companion tonight."

"Yes, Hawk and I have been spending quite a bit of time together," I reply evenly, watching her reaction carefully. I feel Olivia tense beside me, her hand still clasped in mine.

A flicker of annoyance passes across Regina's perfectly made-up face. "Be careful, cousin," she says, her voice honeyed with false concern. "Not everyone is as they appear. Associations can be... risky."

I meet her gaze steadily. "Is that a warning?"

"Just friendly advice," Regina responds, her tone sweet but edged with venom. "One never knows who might be... aligning with unsavory characters."

As she saunters away, her words echo in my mind.

The implication is clear – she's hinting at her alliance with Viktor Kazanov. A chill runs down my spine as I realize the true severity of the threat looming over me.

Olivia squeezes my hand. "What was that about?" she whispers, concern etched on her features.

I force a smile. "Nothing to worry about. Just Regina being Regina."

But Olivia knows me too well to be fooled. "Devin," she says softly, "you know you can tell me anything, right? I'm here for you, always."

For a moment, I'm tempted to unburden myself, to share the weight of the secrets I've been carrying. But I can't risk putting Olivia in danger. So instead, I nod, giving her hand a grateful squeeze. "I know. Thank you."

We make our way toward the restroom, Olivia's presence a comforting warmth beside me. As we turn down a dimly lit corridor, we find our path blocked by Regina and her two cronies, Isabella and Vivian. Their eyes gleam with malicious intent like predators cornering their prey.

"Off to freshen up?" Isabella sneers, her lips curled in a mocking smile.

I feel Olivia stiffen beside me, but I keep my expression neutral. "Is there something you need?" My voice is cool, devoid of emotion.

Vivian smirks, her eyes raking over me dismissively. "We couldn't help but notice how out of place you seem here. Still trying to fit in with the family?"

"It's adorable, really," Regina adds, her voice dripping with condescension. "Playing dress-up doesn't change who you are, Devin."

For a moment, I feel a surge of old insecurities threatening to overwhelm me. But I push them down, drawing strength from the knowledge of who I've become. "And who am I, Regina?" I ask, my voice steady and cold as ice.

"An outsider pretending to be relevant," she spits, her mask of civility slipping.

I take a deep breath, knowing that what I'm about to do will change everything. But I'm done being their punching bag. "Interesting," I say, my voice low and dangerous. "Coming from you, Regina, I suppose you would know all about pretending."

Their smug expressions falter as I continue, my tone remaining unnervingly calm. "Like how you pretend to be the perfect daughter while secretly funneling family funds into personal accounts."

I turn to Isabella, whose eyes have gone wide. "Or how you maintain that happy marriage facade while your 'young male model' friend keeps you company when your husband's away."

Finally, I fix my gaze on Vivian, whose smirk has completely vanished. "And Vivian, those late-night visits to the strip clubs must be exhausting. Does your father know where his precious daughter spends her time?"

The silence that follows is deafening. I can see the shock and fury warring on their faces as they process my words. Beside me, Olivia inhales sharply, her hand moving to intervene. Without looking, I raise my hand slightly, signaling her to stand down. This is my fight, and after years of friendship, she knows when to let me handle things.

"You bitch!" Isabella screeches, her composure shattering. "How dare you—"

"I dare because you came here to intimidate me," I interrupt, my voice still eerily calm. "But I'm not the same girl you used to bully."

Regina's eyes narrow to slits. "You're making a mistake," she hisses, her voice trembling with rage.

Before I can respond, Isabella lunges forward, her hand raised to slap me. I dodge easily, causing her to stumble. Vivian grabs my arm, but I twist free, using a subtle self-defense move to throw her off balance.

"You'll regret this!" Vivian shrieks, her face contorted with fury.

Isabella, regaining her footing, snatches a glass of

wine from a passing server and hurls it at me. I sidestep, and the crimson liquid splashes across Vivian's designer dress instead.

As Vivian howls in outrage, I move swiftly, knocking her clutch from her hands. The contents spill onto the marble floor, including a small vial of pills.

"What's this?" I ask innocently, eyeing the pills. "Something you wouldn't want others to find?"

Isabella charges me again, but I'm ready. I deflect her attack, sending her careening into a nearby table. The crash of shattering glass draws the attention of nearby guests.

Regina, realizing the situation has spiraled out of her control, takes a step back. "This isn't over, Devin," she snarls before turning on her heel and stalking away.

I watch her go, my exterior calm but my insides churning with a mix of satisfaction and simmering rage. As I turn, my eyes lock with Hawk's across the room. He's watching intently.

A few concerned guests approach, but I assure them everything is fine, my voice steady and controlled. As Olivia and I finally make our way to the restroom, she turns to me, her eyes wide.

"Devin, that was... I mean, I knew you could handle yourself, but that was something else," she says, a hint of awe in her voice.

I offer her a small smile. "Sometimes you have to fight fire with fire," I reply softly. "Thanks for having my back."

Olivia squeezes my arm. "Always. But, Devin... there's more going on here than you're telling me, isn't there?"

I meet her gaze in the mirror, seeing the worry etched on her face. For a moment, I consider telling her everything – about Viktor, about the dangers lurking in the shadows. But I can't bring myself to shatter the relative safety of her world.

"It's complicated, Liv," I say finally. "But I promise, I'm handling it."

She nods, though I can see she's not entirely convinced. "Just... be careful, okay? And remember, you're not alone in this. You've got me, and you've got Hawk."

At the mention of Hawk's name, I feel a flutter in my chest. "Speaking of your brother," I say, attempting to lighten the mood, "how much have you been telling him about me?"

Olivia grins, a mischievous glint in her eye. "Only the good stuff, I promise. Well, mostly."

We share a laugh, the tension of the earlier confrontation easing slightly. As we exit the restroom, I steel myself for whatever the rest of the evening might bring. With Olivia by my side and Hawk watching over me, I feel a flicker of hope. Maybe, just maybe, I'm not as alone in this as I thought.

When we return to the main hall, my eyes immediately lock onto Hawk. He's standing rigidly, his expression a mask of cold indifference as Regina places a hand on his arm. The sight sends a fresh wave of anger coursing through me.

Jealousy, hot and fierce, claws at my insides. How dare she touch him? My fingers itch to rip her hand away, to stake my claim. But I force myself to remain outwardly composed even as my mind races with violent possibilities.

I approach them, my strides purposeful. As I draw near, I hear Hawk's icy command: "Do not touch me."

Regina's saccharine voice grates on my nerves. "Oh, come now, Hawk. There's no need to be so distant. We could accomplish so much together."

I position myself beside Hawk, not saying a word but making my presence known. Regina's eyes flick to me, filled with disdain. "Enjoying the party?" she asks, her voice dripping with sarcasm.

I respond by taking a slow sip of my newly acquired wine, holding her gaze steadily over the rim of the glass. The tension between us is palpable. Inside, I'm seething, imagining all the ways I could make Regina regret ever laying eyes on Hawk. But outwardly, I remain a picture of icy composure.

Hawk turns to me, his brow furrowed slightly. "Is everything all right?" he asks, clearly sensing the undercurrents.

Before I can respond, Hawk cuts Regina off. "Regina, I believe this conversation is over," he states firmly. "I'm not interested in any partnership with you."

Regina's smile tightens, a crack in her polished veneer. "Very well. But don't say I didn't offer." She casts a final, venomous glance at me before disappearing into the crowd.

An awkward silence descends. Hawk studies me, concern evident in his eyes. "You seem unsettled," he observes.

I drain my wine in one gulp, the alcohol doing little to calm my frayed nerves. "Just family drama," I reply tersely, my voice betraying none of the turmoil raging within me.

"Do you want to talk about it?" Hawk asks, his voice uncharacteristically gentle.

"No," I say, suddenly feeling suffocated by the opulent surroundings and prying eyes. "I need some air."

Without waiting for a response, I make my way toward the garden, desperate for a moment of solitude.

The cool night air hits me as I step outside, the scent of roses providing a brief respite from the evening's tensions. I take a deep breath, trying to center myself.

As I stare out into the darkness, the distant laughter and music from the party a stark contrast to the turmoil within me, I allow myself a moment of vulnerability. The fear, the anger, the loneliness – it all threatens to overwhelm me. But then I straighten my spine, steeling myself once more.

Suddenly, I feel a presence behind me. Before I can turn, strong hands grasp my waist, spinning me around. My back slams against a cold marble column, knocking the breath from my lungs. Hawk's steel-gray eyes bore into mine, blazing with an intensity that makes my heart race.

"Hawk, what—" I begin, but he cuts me off, his mouth crashing down on mine in a fierce, possessive kiss.

For a split second, I'm frozen in shock. Then, like a dam bursting, all the pent-up frustration and desire I've been holding back explodes. I kiss him back with equal fervor, my fingers tangling in his hair, pulling him closer. Our teeth clash, the kiss more a battle than an embrace.

I bite his lower lip hard enough to draw blood. He growls low in his throat, the sound sending shivers down my spine. His hands roam my body, greedy and demanding as if he's trying to claim every inch of me.

"You're mine, Devin," he rasps against my lips.

The possessiveness in his voice ignites something primal within me. I push back against him, spinning us so that he's the one pressed against the column. My nails rake down his chest, leaving marks even through the fabric of his shirt.

"And you're mine," I snarl, nipping at his jaw. "Don't you ever forget that."

His hand fists in my hair, yanking my head back to expose my throat. He trails hot, open-mouthed kisses down my neck, teeth grazing my pulse point. I can't suppress the moan that escapes me, my body arching into his.

The rush of adrenaline, the thrill of danger – anyone could walk out and see us at any moment – only heightens the intensity of our encounter. It's reckless, it's risky, but in this moment, I don't care. All that matters is Hawk's hands on my body, his lips on my skin driving away every thought of Regina or Viktor and the looming threats that have been haunting me.

Hawk's hand slides up my thigh, pushing the fabric of my dress higher. I gasp as his fingers brush against the sensitive skin of my inner thigh. "Here?" I pant, equal parts scandalized and thrilled.

He pulls back slightly, his eyes dark with desire. "Tell me to stop," he challenges, his voice rough.

I meet his gaze defiantly. "Don't you dare."

A wicked smile curves his lips before he claims my mouth again. His touch is fire, burning away everything but this moment, this raw, primal connection between us.

In the back of my mind, I know this is dangerous – not just the risk of discovery, but the way I'm losing myself in him. Hawk Rivers is becoming my addiction, my obsession. But as his hands and lips work their magic, I can't bring myself to care. For now, I let myself get lost in the sensations and in the dark, twisted passion we share.

Eventually, we pull apart, both of us breathing heavily. Hawk rests his forehead against mine, his thumb tracing my swollen lips. "You drive me crazy," he murmurs.

I smirk, nipping at his finger. "Likewise."

For a moment, we stand there in silence, the air around us charged with unspoken emotions and lingering desire. Then, reality begins to seep back in. I can hear the muffled sounds of the party, a reminder of where we are and the roles we're supposed to be playing.

Hawk seems to sense the shift in my mood. He cups

my face in his hands, his touch surprisingly gentle after the intensity of our encounter. "Whatever's going on, Devin, whatever you're hiding – you don't have to face it alone. I'm here. Let me in."

For a heartbeat, I'm tempted. The weight of my secrets feels crushing, and the idea of sharing that burden is tantalizing. But I can't. Not yet.

I place my hand over his, allowing myself a moment of vulnerability. "I know," I say softly. "Just... give me time."

He studies me for a long moment before nodding. "All right. But remember, I'm not a patient man, Devin. And I don't like being kept in the dark."

There's a warning in his tone that sends a shiver down my spine – equal parts fear and excitement. I know I'm playing a dangerous game, keeping secrets from a man like Hawk Rivers. But it's a game I have to play, at least for now.

I straighten my dress and run a hand through my hair, trying to erase the evidence of our passionate encounter. Hawk does the same, adjusting his tie and smoothing down his jacket.

As we prepare to rejoin the party, I catch my reflection in a nearby window. My lips are swollen, my eyes bright with lingering desire.

FIFTEEN

From my office atop Rivers Financial, I survey my domain, feeling the weight of power and the constant threat of those who would take it from me. The gentle hum of technology surrounds me, a reminder of the control I wield and the precarious nature of that control.

A soft knock breaks my reverie. "Come in," I command, not turning from the window.

Daniel enters, his footsteps barely audible on the plush carpet. "Hawk, I have the information you requested," he says, his tone familiar yet respectful.

I turn, eyeing the tablet in his hands. "Show me."

Daniel activates the screen, and a series of images and reports flicker to life. I lean in, my eyes narrowing as I take in the damning evidence. Regina Black and Viktor

Kazanov, caught in clandestine meetings, their alliance laid bare before me.

"They've been coordinating for months," Daniel explains, his tone grim. "Financial transactions, shared resources—their alliance is solidified."

I feel a tightening in my chest, a mix of anger and anticipation. "Regina and Viktor together amplify each other's influence," I muse, more to myself than to Daniel. "This changes everything."

Daniel nods. "Their combined efforts could disrupt your operations significantly."

"We need more," I decide, my mind already racing. "Contact Sphinx. I want everything they can dig up on Regina and Viktor's operations. And while you're at it, see if you can get any leads on Sphinx's identity. I want to know why they've been helping us."

Daniel raises an eyebrow. "You think Sphinx will cooperate?"

"They will if we make it worth their while," I reply coldly. "Offer whatever it takes. I need that information."

As Daniel leaves to make the arrangements, I turn to my intercom. "Lucas, arrange a private dinner for tonight with Regina Black. Use the pretext of discussing a potential business merger. Book us at La Sorella."

"Right away, sir," Lucas responds promptly.

As I prepare for the encounter, I review everything I know about Regina—her tactics, her weaknesses, her desires. I select my attire with care, a tailored suit that speaks of power and control. Every detail matters in this game we play.

La Sorella is a sanctuary of luxury and discretion, the perfect backdrop for the dance of deception I'm about to engage in. I arrive early, selecting a private dining room with a view of the city. The muted lighting casts long shadows, perfect for hiding truths and revealing lies.

Regina enters, a vision of elegance and ambition. Her smile is dazzling, but her eyes are sharp, ever-watchful. "Hawk, it's delightful to see you," she greets, extending her hand.

I take it, my grip firm and cold. "Regina. Sit."

As we settle in and the first course is served, I begin to weave my web. "I'm sure you're wondering why I've called this meeting," I start, my voice level and controlled.

Regina's eyes light up with interest. "I assumed it was to discuss the potential merger you mentioned. Our combined resources could position us to dominate in ways we've only dreamed of."

I lean back, fixing her with a steely gaze. "Let's cut

the bullshit, Regina. I know about your alliance with Viktor Kazanov."

Her composure slips for just a moment, a flicker of shock crossing her face before she regains control. "I don't know what you're talking about," she says smoothly.

"Don't insult my intelligence," I reply, my voice sharp as a blade. "I warned you what would happen if you ever threatened Devin again. And yet, at the family event, you couldn't help yourself, could you?"

Regina's eyes narrow. "Devin is a big girl. She can handle a little family drama."

I lean forward, my voice dropping to a dangerous whisper. "Let me be very clear. Anyone who hurts Devin will pay. And that includes you, Regina. Your little alliance with Viktor? It ends now."

"Or what?" Regina challenges, though I can see the fear creeping into her eyes.

I smile, cold and predatory. "Or I'll destroy everything you've built. Your reputation, your business, your standing in the family. I'll leave you with nothing."

Regina's face pales, but she quickly recovers. "You're bluffing. You don't have that kind of power."

I laugh at her stupidity. She still doesn't realize who she's dealing with.

"Are you willing to bet everything on that?" I ask softly.

A tense silence falls between us. Finally, Regina speaks. "What do you want from me?"

"A partnership," I reply, watching her carefully. "A real one. You'll feed me information on Viktor's operations. In return, I'll protect you from the fallout when we take him down."

Regina's eyes widen in surprise. "You want to take down Viktor?"

I nod. "And you're going to help me do it. Consider it your penance for crossing me."

As we hammer out the details of our arrangement, I can see the calculations running behind Regina's eyes. She's looking for an angle, a way to turn this to her advantage. I want her to try. I'll be ready.

The drive back to my penthouse gives me time to process the evening's events, to strategize my next move. But as I step into the dimly lit space, I sense a shift in the air. Tension, thick and palpable.

Devin stands by the window, her silhouette stark against the city lights. She doesn't turn as I enter, but I can feel the weight of her gaze.

"You're home late," she remarks, her voice unnaturally calm.

I approach cautiously, aware of the minefield I'm walking into. "The meeting ran longer than expected."

Now she turns, and I'm struck by the coldness in her eyes. Her face is a mask of indifference, but I can see the slight tremor in her hands. She's furious.

"I know you were with Regina," she states, her tone level but laced with an undercurrent of rage.

"It was a business meeting. Necessary to address certain issues."

"Issues that require private dinners?" she asks, her voice still eerily calm. "What else did you discuss?"

The tension between us crackles like electricity. I find myself both concerned and intrigued by her controlled anger. This is a side of Devin I haven't seen before.

"I was gathering information to protect us," I explain, moving closer to her. "Regina and Viktor have formed an alliance. I needed to confront her directly. To set up a way to interfere."

Devin's eyes flash with something—Interest? It's gone too quickly for me to be sure. "And did you get what you needed?" she asks.

I nod, reaching out to brush a strand of hair from her face. She doesn't flinch away, but I can feel the tension radiating from her body. "I did. Regina will be feeding us information on Viktor's operations. I'm sure she'll try to turn things to her advantage and try to screw us at some point, but we'll handle that when we get there."

A small smile curves Devin's lips, cold and dangerous. "Okay," she says simply. "Are you seeking any additional resources?"

I watch her, but her gaze gives nothing away. "I am."

We're standing so close now I can feel the heat radiating from her body. "You're jealous," I observe quietly.

Her eyes meet mine, unflinching. "I am."

I lean in slightly, my voice softening. "You need to understand that I would never betray your trust."

Devin places a hand on my chest, and I can't tell if she's pushing me away or pulling me closer. "Actions speak louder than words," she replies.

"Then let me show you," I whisper, closing the final inches between us. I curl my hand around her throat and hold her there, tilting her head up.

Our lips meet in a kiss that's equal parts passion and frustration. It's a battle for dominance, neither of us willing to yield.

"This doesn't excuse keeping me in the dark," Devin says, her voice husky. She pulls out of my grasp and takes two steps back. Away from me. She dared to pull away.

I yank her to me again, crushing my lips against hers. She responds immediately, her kisses as fierce and angry as they are passionate. Her nails dig into my back, and I grip her hips hard enough to bruise.

We break apart, both breathing heavily. "Stop hiding from me," I growl, my voice low and rough.

Devin's eyes meet mine, a challenge burning in their depths. "Are you sure you can handle that, Hawk?" she asks, her tone both mocking and seductive.

I respond by pushing her against the window, the cool glass a stark contrast to the heat of our bodies. "Try me," I whisper against her neck.

As we lose ourselves in a tangle of limbs and heated kisses, I can't help but marvel at the woman in my arms. Devin is a force of nature, as dangerous and unpredictable as she is alluring. And as I give in to the dark passion between us, I am reminded of a crucial fact, I've finally met my match.

SIXTEEN

The city's neon glow fades behind me as I slip deeper into the shadows of a forgotten alleyway. My heart races, not from fear but from the exhilaration of momentary freedom. Hawk's security detail, while necessary, has become suffocating. This clandestine excursion to purchase a personal item feels like stealing air after being underwater for too long.

I pull my hood lower, relishing the anonymity it provides. The cool night air caresses my face, carrying with it the scents of the city – a heady mixture of car exhaust, street food, and rain-slicked pavement. For a moment, I'm just another face in the crowd, invisible and unremarkable.

But invisibility is an illusion, and one I've clearly overestimated.

The first prickle of unease crawls up my spine as I round a corner into a narrower street. The hairs on the back of my neck stand on end, a primal warning system alerting me to unseen eyes. I quicken my pace, the soft tap of my footsteps echoing off brick walls. Behind me, other footfalls join the rhythm – too steady, too purposeful to be casual passers-by.

I risk a glance over my shoulder. Shadows detach themselves from doorways, solidifying into hulking figures that match my stride. My pulse quickens, adrenaline flooding my system. I've walked into a trap, and the jaws are about to snap shut.

Ahead, the alley narrows further. Two more men materialize, blocking my path. Their broad shoulders and hard eyes leave no doubt – these are Viktor Kazanov's men. The tattoos peeking out from beneath their collars confirm it.

I don't hesitate. Survival instinct takes over, my body moving before my mind can fully process the danger. I pivot, driving my knee up into the closest thug's groin. As he doubles over, I use his momentum to propel myself forward, aiming for the gap between him and his companion.

But they're prepared for resistance. Hands grab at my clothing, meaty fingers digging into my arms. I twist, breaking one hold only to find myself ensnared by another. My martial arts training kicks in, muscle memory taking over as I deliver precise strikes to vulnerable points – throats, solar plexuses, insteps.

For a moment, I gain the upper hand. Bodies crumple around me, groans of pain filling the air. But there are too many of them, the confined space working against me. A blunt object – a pipe, perhaps – connects with the back of my head. Pain explodes across my skull, my vision blurring at the edges.

I stagger, fighting to maintain consciousness. Rough hands seize me, forcing my arms behind my back. The plastic bite of zip ties cuts into my wrists.

"You're coming with us," a gravelly voice growls in my ear.

I struggle, but the world is spinning, darkness encroaching on my vision. The last thing I register is the acrid smell of van upholstery before oblivion claims me.

CONSCIOUSNESS RETURNS SLOWLY, dragging me back to a reality I'd rather avoid. The first thing I notice is the cold – a bone-deep chill that seeps through my clothes. Then comes the discomfort – arms pulled tightly behind me, ankles secured to the legs of what feels like a metal chair. My head throbs, a dull ache pulsing in time with my heartbeat.

I force my eyes open, blinking against the harsh glare of fluorescent lights. As my vision clears, the details of my prison come into focus. An abandoned warehouse, vast and decrepit. Rusted metal beams stretch overhead, disappearing into shadows. Broken windows let in slivers of moonlight, creating eerie patterns on the concrete floor. The air is thick with the scent of mildew and stagnant water.

Immediately, my mind kicks into overdrive, assessing the situation with cold precision. I catalog potential weapons, escape routes, structural weaknesses. The chair I'm bound to – old, but sturdy. The zip ties – tight, but not unbreakable. A discarded nail glints on the floor, just within reach if I can maneuver carefully.

Footsteps echo in the cavernous space, growing louder. I school my features into a mask of indifference, determined not to show weakness. A figure emerges from the gloom, and my stomach clenches with a mixture of anger and disgust.

Regina. My second cousin, my lifelong rival, and now, apparently, my captor.

She circles me like a shark scenting blood, a smug smile playing on her perfectly painted lips. "Comfortable?" she asks, her voice dripping with false concern.

I meet her gaze steadily, injecting as much derision into my tone as possible. "Is this your way of hosting a family reunion? I must say, your event planning skills leave something to be desired."

Regina's laugh is cold, devoid of any real mirth. "Always so witty. I see Hawk's taste hasn't improved much."

At the mention of Hawk's name, I feel a flicker of possessiveness, quickly suppressed. I won't give her the satisfaction of seeing any reaction. Instead, I arch an eyebrow, my voice laced with contempt. "Jealousy doesn't suit you, Regina. Is kidnapping your new hobby? It seems a bit... pedestrian for someone of your supposed stature."

Her eyes flash with irritation, a crack in her polished veneer. "You think you're clever, but you're in over your head. You have no idea what forces you're dealing with."

I almost laugh at the cliché. "Oh please, spare me the melodrama. Viktor may be a thug, but he's hardly the mastermind you're making him out to be."

Regina's eyes widen almost imperceptibly. I've struck a nerve.

Yeah, I know. Viktor's not the mastermind Regina thinks he is. But finding the one backing him has taken me years and I'm closer than ever.

She leans in closer, her breath hot against my ear. "Did Hawk ever tell you about our history?"

I roll my eyes, not bothering to hide my disdain.

"Your delusions are showing, Regina. What's next? Are you going to tell me that you and Hawk had some torrid love affair? Please. I know him far better than you ever did or will."

"We were close once," Regina continues, her voice silky smooth but with an undercurrent of desperation. "Very close. You were just a convenient distraction."

The lie is so transparent it's almost insulting. I know Hawk and the depth of his disdain for Regina. A part of me wants to lash out, to defend what Hawk and I have. But I push that impulse down. Emotional detachment is key here.

I smirk, allowing a hint of pity to color my tone. "If that's true, why are you so threatened by me? Face it, Regina. Hawk never wanted you. Not when we were younger, and certainly not now. You're just a sad, desperate woman clinging to a fantasy."

Regina's facade crumbles, rage contorting her features. "You little bitch," she snarls, her hand raises and she slaps me across the face. "I'm not threatened by a pathetic little girl playing at being a woman."

I laugh, the sound cold and mocking. "Really? Then why go to all this trouble? Face it, Regina. You're terrified that I've succeeded where you've always failed. Hawk sees me as an equal, a partner. You? You're not even a blip on his radar."

Regina's composure shatters. She grabs my hair, yanking my head back painfully. "You think you're so special? You have no idea what's coming. Viktor has plans that will destroy everything you and Hawk have built. And when it's all over, I'll be there to pick up the pieces."

I meet her gaze unflinchingly, a predatory smile curving my lips. "Thank you for confirming my suspicions, Regina. You always were too easy to manipulate."

Confusion flickers across her face, quickly replaced by horror as she realizes her mistake. She's revealed far more than she intended.

"You won't be so smug once Viktor arrives," she hisses, trying to regain control of the situation. "He has plans for you that will make you wish you'd never crossed us."

I lean forward as much as my restraints allow, my voice low and dangerous. "Bring it on. Viktor's just another obstacle to be overcome. And whoever's backing him? They've made a fatal error in underestimating me. I've been working for years to uncover the truth, and you've just handed me another piece of the puzzle."

Regina's eyes widen, fear replacing anger. She opens her mouth to speak, but no words come out.

I press my advantage. "Run along now, Regina. Go report to your master like a good dog."

Regina backs away, her composure in tatters. "We'll see," she manages to spit out before turning and fleeing from the room.

As her footsteps fade, I immediately begin working the zip tie against the nail I spotted earlier. The abrasive surface starts to fray the plastic, but progress is agonizingly slow. I grit my teeth, focusing on the task at hand rather than the implications of what I've learned.

Time becomes fluid, measured only by the steady drip of water from a leaking pipe and the rasp of plastic against metal. My mind races, piecing together the fragments of information I've gathered over the years. Viktor is just the tip of the iceberg. There's a larger conspiracy at play, one that threatens Hawk and I won't allow that. Nobody hurts my man.

The distant rumble of an engine shatters the silence. Voices echo through the warehouse – Viktor's men are drawing closer. My heart rate spikes, fingers working furiously at the restraints.

Just as panic threatens to overtake me, I feel the zip tie give way. A surge of triumph courses through me as I free my hands, quickly working to release my ankles. I may be outnumbered and unarmed, but I'm far from helpless. I take a few steps and start to feel optimistic until a group of men walk in and surround me. Fuck!

SEVENTEEN

The shattered vase lies scattered across the polished floor of my penthouse, each jagged piece a stark reminder of my failure. My eyes narrow as I replay the security footage, watching Devin slip away from her guards like a shadow melting into darkness. Fury builds within me, a cold, calculated rage directed not just at her captors, but at the incompetent fools I'd trusted with her safety.

"Find them," I snarl at Daniel, my voice low and deadly. "Every last one of those guards. I want them brought to me."

Daniel nods, his face grim. "Already on it. But Hawk, there's something else you need to see."

He pulls up another feed, and I watch as a nondescript van intercepts Devin moments after she evades her security detail. The efficiency of the operation speaks volumes. This was planned, coordinated. My hands clench into fists, knuckles white with suppressed rage.

"Regina," I growl, the name tasting like poison on my tongue. That snake dared to touch what's mine. I'd been playing a long game with her, letting her think she had a chance, all to uncover her connection to Kazanov. But she crossed a line, and now? Now, she'll pay with her life.

"Mobilize everyone," I order, my voice cutting through the air like a blade. "I want every resource and contact we have working on this. Find her. Now."

As my team springs into action, I retreat to my private armory. Each weapon I select is a promise - of vengeance, of retribution. The familiar weight of my custom Glock settles into my palm, a cold comfort.

My phone buzzes - it's Max, Sphinx's enigmatic assistant. "We've located her," Max's voice crackles through the secure line. "Warehouse district. Sending coordinates now."

Relief floods through me, quickly replaced by a laser-focused determination. "I'm on my way. Keep me updated on any movement."

The drive to the warehouse is a blur of city lights and strategic planning. I brief my team, my voice steady despite the storm raging inside me. "Primary objective is Devin's extraction. Secondary objective is the elimination of all threats. Regina and Kazanov are mine."

As we approach the target, the scale of the operation becomes clear. Kazanov's men swarm the area like ants, heavily armed and on high alert. A savage smile twists my lips. Good. Let them try to stop me.

"On my mark," I murmur into the comms as we take our positions. The night air is thick with tension, the calm before the storm. "Three. Two. One. Execute."

The world erupts into chaos. Gunfire shatters the silence, muzzle flashes illuminating the darkness in staccato bursts. I move with cold precision, each shot finding its mark with deadly accuracy. Bodies fall around me, but I barely register them. They're obstacles, nothing more.

"East wing clear," Daniel's voice crackles in my ear. "Heavy resistance in the north sector."

I change direction, cutting through the warehouse like a scythe through wheat. Two of Kazanov's men round a corner, their eyes widening in recognition. They don't even have time to raise their weapons before I put them down.

A burst of gunfire forces me into cover. I peek around the corner, counting targets. Five of them, well-positioned. A grenade rolls from my hand, the explosion sending shrapnel and bodies flying. I'm moving before the dust settles, stepping over the carnage without a second glance.

"Boss," Daniel's voice is tight with urgency. "We've got eyes on the primary target. Southeast corner, upper level. Regina and Kazanov are with her."

My blood runs cold at the thought of Devin in their hands. "On my way. Secure the perimeter, no one gets out alive."

I take the stairs three at a time, my heartbeat thundering in my ears. The door to the upper level looms before me, a final barrier between me and my goal. With a nod to Daniel, who's appeared at my side, we breach.

The scene before me ignites a fury I've never known. Devin, bound to a chair, her eyes blazing with defiance. Regina, her face twisted in a sneer of triumph. And Kazanov, his gun pressed against Devin's temple.

"Ah, Hawk," Kazanov's voice drips with false cordiality. "So good of you to join us. We were just discussing the future of your empire."

"The only future you need to worry about is the next five minutes," I reply, my voice arctic. "Let her go, and I might make it quick."

Regina laughs, the sound grating on my nerves. "Oh, Hawk. Always so dramatic. Did you really think I'd let you play me for a fool? This little bitch has been a thorn in my side for far too long."

I see Devin's eyes narrow at Regina's words, but right now, my entire focus is on getting Devin out alive.

"Last chance," I warn, my gun trained steadily on Kazanov. "Release her."

Instead of complying, Kazanov tightens his grip on Devin, using her as a shield. "I don't think so. You see, Ms. West here has some very valuable information. Information that could bring your entire world crashing down."

I don't let his words faze me. My eyes lock with Devin's, and in that moment, a silent communication passes between us. I see the trust there, the understanding. She gives me an almost imperceptible nod.

"You're right, Kazanov," I say, my tone shifting. "Someone does have valuable information." My gaze flicks to Regina. "And she's outlived her usefulness."

Several things happen at once. Devin throws her weight backward, knocking Kazanov off balance. I fire, the bullet grazing his shoulder and causing him to lose his grip. Daniel surges forward, tackling Regina before she can reach for her weapon.

I'm on Kazanov in an instant, my fist connecting

with his jaw with a satisfying crunch. He staggers but recovers quickly, lashing out with a vicious right hook. I feel the impact, tasting blood, but the pain only fuels my rage.

We grapple, trading blows. Kazanov is strong, but I'm faster, more focused. Every punch I land is for Devin, for the fear she must have felt, for every second she was in danger because of this man.

From the corner of my eye, I see Daniel subduing Regina, efficiently zip-tying her hands behind her back. Devin has managed to work one hand free and is struggling with her bonds.

Kazanov sees it too and makes a desperate lunge for his fallen gun. I intercept him, driving my knee into his solar plexus. As he doubles over, gasping for air, I grab him by the throat and slam him against the wall.

"I told you," I growl, my face inches from his, "this ends now."

I see the fear in his eyes, the realization that he's lost. It's a look I've seen many times in the boardroom, but never with such satisfaction.

"Hawk," Devin's voice cuts through the haze of my anger. I turn to see her standing, rubbing her wrists where the ropes had chafed her skin. Her eyes meet mine, a mix of relief and something deeper, more complex. "We need them alive. For now."

I hesitate for a moment, every fiber of my being wanting to end Kazanov's miserable life right here. But Devin's right. We need information, and dead men can't talk.

With a frustrated growl, I slam Kazanov's head against the wall, knocking him unconscious. He crumples to the floor, and I turn my full attention to Devin.

In two strides, I'm at her side, my hands cupping her face, eyes searching for any sign of injury. "Are you hurt?" I demand, my voice rough with emotion.

She shakes her head, a small smile on her face despite the situation. "I'm fine. Your timing is impeccable as always, Mr. Rivers."

The relief that washes over me is almost overwhelming. I pull her close, inhaling her scent, feeling the warmth of her body against mine. For a moment, the world narrows to just us, the chaos around us fading into the background.

"Don't ever do that to me again," I murmur into her hair, my arms tightening around her.

She pulls back slightly, her eyes meeting mine with that familiar spark of defiance. "Do what? Get kidnapped? I'll try to pencil that in less often."

Despite everything, I feel a chuckle rumble in my chest. Even in the face of danger, her spirit remains unbroken. It's one of the things I admire most about her.

Our moment is interrupted by Daniel clearing his throat. "Boss, we need to move. Local authorities will be here soon, and we have some... cleaning up to do."

I nod, reluctantly releasing Devin but keeping a hand on the small of her back. "Secure Kazanov and Regina. We'll take them to the secondary location for questioning."

As my team efficiently carries out my orders, I turn back to Devin. "We have a lot to discuss," I say, my tone serious.

She meets my gaze steadily. "Yes, we do. But not here, not now."

I nod in agreement. There will be time for explanations, for unraveling the web of secrets and lies that led us to this point. For now, I'm content knowing she's safe and back where she belongs — by my side.

As we make our way out of the warehouse, the cool night air hits us, carrying with it the promise of a new dawn. The city sprawls before us, unaware of the drama that unfolded in its shadows. But I know that after tonight, nothing will be the same.

I guide Devin toward one of the waiting SUVs, my hand never leaving her back. As we settle into the vehicle, I catch her watching me, a mix of emotions playing across her face.

"What?" I ask, raising an eyebrow.

She shakes her head slightly, a small smile tugging on her lips. "Nothing. Just... thank you. For coming for me."

I reach out, taking her hand in mine, my thumb tracing circles on her skin. "Always," I promise, my voice low and intense. "I will always come for you, Devin."

As the car pulls away from the warehouse, leaving behind the chaos and violence, I feel a shift in the air between us. The game we've been playing, the dance of power and control, has changed. We've crossed a line tonight, and there's no going back.

But as I look at Devin, her head resting against the seat, eyes closed in exhaustion but her hand still firmly in mine, I realize I don't want to go back.

The city lights smudge past the window as we drive, and I allow myself a moment of contentment. Devin is safe. Kazanov and Regina are neutralized. And tomorrow... tomorrow I figure out who the mastermind behind every attack on my business and life is.

As we near my penthouse, Devin stirs, her eyes opening to meet mine. There's a vulnerability there that I've never seen mixed with her usual strength. It's a heady combination.

"Hawk," she says softly, her voice barely above a whisper. "What happens now?"

I squeeze her hand gently, my gaze never leaving hers. "Now, we rest. Tomorrow, we plan. And then…"

"And then?" she prompts, a hint of her usual challenge in her tone.

A slow smile spreads across my face, all threat. "And then, my dear, we conquer."

EIGHTEEN

The warehouse looms before us, a hulking metal beast on the outskirts of the city. As Hawk pulls the car to a stop, I feel a thrill of anticipation mixed with dread. Today, we get answers.

Hawk's hand finds mine, squeezing gently. "Ready?" he asks, his voice low and dangerous.

I meet his gaze, seeing my own ruthless determination reflected there. "Yes."

The interior of the warehouse is cold and damp, our footsteps echoing off concrete walls. In the center of the vast space, two figures are bound to chairs - Regina and Kazanov, both looking worse for wear after a night in captivity.

Hawk's men stand guard, their faces impassive. As

we approach, I see Regina's eyes widen, a flicker of hope crossing her features.

"Hawk," she starts, her voice hoarse. "Please, you have to understand—"

Hawk cuts her off with a sharp gesture. "Understand what, Regina? That you betrayed me? That you put Devin in danger?" His voice is ice, devoid of any warmth. "Oh, I understand perfectly."

I watch as Hawk circles Kazanov like a predator stalking its prey. The crime lord tries to maintain his bravado, but I see the fear in his eyes. He knows what's coming.

"You made a grave mistake, Kazanov," Hawk says, his tone conversational despite the menace underlying his words. "You touched what's mine."

Before Kazanov can respond, Hawk's fist connects with his jaw in a vicious uppercut. The crack of bone is audible, and blood sprays from Kazanov's mouth.

I feel a rush of savage pleasure at the sight. This man who thought he could use me as a pawn in his game is about to learn the cost of his arrogance.

Hawk doesn't stop with one punch. His fists rain down on Kazanov in a brutal onslaught, each impact punctuated by a grunt of exertion. I watch, mesmerized, as Hawk unleashes his fury. It's addicting. Watching the power behind his fury is so fucking sexy.

When he finally steps back, Kazanov is barely recognizable, his face a swollen mass of bruises and blood. Hawk's knuckles are split and bleeding, but he doesn't seem to notice.

"Now," Hawk says, wiping his hands on a handkerchief, "let's talk about who you're working for."

Kazanov spits out a mouthful of blood and broken teeth. "Go to hell," he manages to slur.

A cold smile spreads across Hawk's face. "We're already there." In one fluid motion, he pulls out a wicked-looking knife. The blade glints in the harsh fluorescent light as he brings it to Kazanov's hand - the same hand he used to grab me during my captivity.

"Fuck you," Kazanov mumbles.

"Wrong answer," Hawk growls, and with a swift movement, he drives the knife through Kazanov's palm and into the wooden arm of the chair. "This is for daring to touch my woman."

Kazanov's scream echoes through the warehouse, raw and agonized. I should feel horrified, but all I feel is a grim satisfaction. This is justice served cold and brutal.

"Hawk, please!" Regina's desperate voice breaks through the tension. "I can explain everything. We can work this out. You know me."

Something in me snaps. I whirl on Regina, my hand connecting with her face in a resounding slap. "Shut up," I hiss, leaning in close. "You don't get to beg. You don't get to manipulate. Not anymore. And not my man."

Regina's eyes widen in shock, a red mark blooming on her cheek where I struck her. For once, she's silent.

I turn back to Kazanov, who's breathing heavily, his eyes glazed with pain. "You want to know something interesting?" I ask, my voice deceptively calm and low. "I'm the only person who can get to the Sphinx."

Kazanov's head snaps up, disbelief warring with fear in his bloodshot eyes. "You're lying," he chokes out.

I lean in, close enough to smell the coppery scent of his blood. "Am I? Do you really want to take that chance? Because I can make your entire life and family history disappear with a few keystrokes. Your money, your properties, your family's wealth, your precious reputation - all of it... gone."

"You don't have that kind of power," Kazanov spits, but I hear the uncertainty in his voice.

I smile, cold and dangerous. "Want to find out?"

Kazanov's composure finally breaks. He lunges forward as much as his bonds will allow, spewing a stream of obscenities and threats. "I'll kill you!" he roars. "I'll tear you apart with my bare hands, you fucking bitch!"

I step back, unfazed by his outburst. "One last

chance, Kazanov. Tell me who's really behind the attacks on Rivers Financial, or I promise you, your family will be drowning in debt and poverty long after you're dead."

For a long moment, the only sound in the warehouse is Kazanov's ragged breathing. Then, finally, he slumps in defeat.

"I don't know who it is," he admits in a croak. "But I know it's someone in the Rivers family."

I exchange a glance with Hawk. We both expected this but neither wanted to say it. The implications are staggering.

Hawk moves to my side, his hand coming to rest possessively at the small of my back. "You've been very helpful, Kazanov," he says, his voice silky smooth. "Now, I'm afraid our business is concluded."

With a nod to one of his men, Hawk guides me toward the exit. As we walk away, I hear the distinct sound of a gun being cocked.

"Wait," I say, turning back. "I want to see this."

Hawk's eyes search mine for a moment before he nods. "Very well."

We watch as Hawk's man raises his weapon, aiming first at Kazanov, then at Regina. Two shots ring out in quick succession, the sound reverberating off the warehouse walls.

As the echoes fade, I feel a weight lift from my shoulders. Two down. One to go.

Hawk's arm wraps around my waist, pulling me close. I lean into him, feeling the solid warmth of his body against mine. I just want to rub myself all over him at this moment.

"Are you okay?" he asks softly, his lips brushing my ear.

I look up at him, taking in the intensity of his gaze, the splatters of blood on his crisp white shirt. In this moment, covered in the evidence of his ruthlessness, he's never been more attractive to me.

"I'm perfect," I reply, reaching up to pull him into a fierce kiss.

As we break apart, breathless, Hawk's eyes are dark with desire and something deeper, more possessive. "Let's go home," he growls.

I nod, a shiver of anticipation running down my spine.

NINETEEN

I'm just about to step into the shower when I hear Devin's voice, low and authoritative, coming from the bedroom. Curiosity piqued, I wrap a towel around my waist and move silently towards the door.

"Max, I need you to pull all the details on Hawk's immediate family," Devin says, her tone crisp and professional. "Kazanov mentioned someone in the Rivers family is backing him. I'm going to check on the family finances, see who has the need to remove Hawk to take over."

I lean against the doorframe, watching her. She's pacing, still gloriously naked from our earlier activities, her hair a wild tangle around her shoulders. Even like this – or perhaps especially like this – she exudes power and control.

"Yes, boss," a male voice responds from the phone. "I'll have the information to you within the hour."

"Good. Keep me updated on any changes," Devin says before ending the call.

She turns, finally noticing me. For a moment, I see a flicker of uncertainty in her eyes, quickly replaced by resolve. She knows I've heard everything, and she's waiting for my reaction.

I don't give her one. Instead, I simply raise an eyebrow, waiting.

Devin takes a deep breath. "Max is my assistant," she says, her voice steady. "I'm part of the Hacker Alliance."

In three long strides, I'm across the room. I pin her against the wall, my hand at her throat. It's not a tight grip – I'd never hurt her – but it's enough to assert my dominance. "I know that already," I say, my voice low and dangerous. "Is there anything else you'd like to share?"

I can see the conflict in her eyes, the struggle between her instinct for secrecy and her desire to let me in. Finally, she makes her decision.

"I'm Sphinx," she says, her voice barely above a whisper.

For a moment, I'm frozen. Well, that answers who has been helping the company and why. Then, I feel a smile tugging my lips. Before I know it, I'm chuckling, pulling her into my arms and kissing her deeply.

Devin pulls back, confusion written across her face. "What's so funny?"

I lead her to the sofa, settling her on my lap. "When you told Kazanov you were the only one who could reach Sphinx, I was worried there was another man I'd have to kill," I admit.

She rolls her eyes, but I can see the hint of a smile. "You know I'm not involved with anyone else," she says. "There was no need for those thoughts."

"You're mine, Devin," I growl, tightening my grip on her waist. "The thought of anyone else touching you, knowing you like I do... it drives me insane."

Her eyes darken with desire, and she leans in to nip at my jaw. "Likewise," she murmurs. "I don't share what's mine, Hawk. And you are very much *mine*."

The possessiveness in her voice sends a thrill through me. I capture her lips in a fierce kiss, pouring all my hunger, my need, my obsession into it.

"Tell me more," I urge gently, running my fingers through her hair.

Devin takes a deep breath. "I created the Hacker Alliance when I was twelve," she says, her voice soft. "I wanted to make friends, but with my... social awkwardness, it was hard. That was the only way to meet people like me."

I nod, encouraging her to continue.

"Of course, I had abilities that none of my members had," she says, a hint of pride in her voice. "It allowed me to be the best in the world. But..." she hesitates, her fingers tracing patterns on my chest. "I always felt alone in my family. Even though everyone showed me love, they still treated me like a little freak. Nobody else was a genius, nobody else could use code like I did, or deal with numbers, or had an eidetic memory."

I tighten my arms around her, offering silent support.

"When it came to all that, I felt completely comfortable," Devin continues. "But dealing with people was hard. Having Olivia always felt like a blessing, but even with her, I still held back. I wasn't sure how she would react to the emotional disconnect I have with most people."

I consider her words carefully before responding. "Olivia became your friend in second grade," I remind her gently. "She's always loved you for being yourself, not for anything else. You should feel comfortable opening up to her, but only if you want."

Devin looks up at me, her eyes shining with unshed tears. "How do you know that?" she asks.

I smile, brushing a strand of hair from her face. "I make it my business to know everything about the people I care about," I say. "And you, Devin West, are the only person I truly care about. The only one who matters."

She inhales sharply at my admission. "Hawk..."

I press a finger to her lips. "Let me finish," I say softly. "You're not alone anymore, Devin. You don't have to hide who you are, not from me. I see you – all of you – and I want every part."

Devin's eyes search mine, and whatever she finds there seems to satisfy her. She nods, then settles more comfortably against my chest. "Your turn," she says. "Tell me about your family."

I sigh, resting my chin on top of her head. "It's not a happy story," I warn her.

"I'm not here for happy stories," she retorts. "I'm here for you."

Her words warm something deep inside me. I take a deep breath and begin.

"I took control of Rivers Financial right out of college," I say. "My mother had died a few years earlier, and my father... he couldn't cope. He spiraled, lost himself in drinking and bad investments. The company was my mother's creation, her legacy. I couldn't let it fall apart."

Devin's hand finds mine, squeezing gently. "That must have been hard," she murmurs.

I nod. "It was. My uncle – my father's brother – tried to fight me for control. Said I was too young, too inexperienced. But the board sided with me. They knew my mother had been grooming me for this since I was a child."

"Your uncle," Devin says thoughtfully. "Could he be behind this?"

"It's possible," I admit. "He's never forgiven me for 'stealing' what he saw as his. But he's not the only possibility."

Devin shifts, looking up at me. "Your father?"

I meet her gaze, seeing the sharp intelligence there. "Yes," I say. "He's been pressuring me for years to sell the company, to give him more money for his... habits. I've always refused."

"And now he might be working with Kazanov to force your hand," Devin finishes.

I nod grimly. "It's a possibility we can't ignore."

Devin's eyes harden with determination. "We'll find out who's behind this, Hawk. I promise you that. And when we do..."

"We'll destroy them," I finish, a cold smile on my face. "Together."

She matches my smile with one of her own, equally dangerous. "Together," she agrees.

I pull her in for another kiss, fierce and possessive. When we break apart, I rest my forehead against hers. "You know," I say softly, "I never thought I'd find someone who could match me. Someone who could understand the darkness inside me, the need for control, for power."

Devin's hand comes up to cup my cheek. "I understand it because I feel it too," she says. "You're not alone either, Hawk. You haven't been for six years."

"Neither have you."

"We should get to work," Devin says after a moment, though she makes no move to leave my lap. "We have a mastermind to find."

I nod, but I can't resist stealing one more kiss. "Five more minutes," I murmur against her lips.

She laughs softly, the sound sending shivers down my spine. "Five minutes," she agrees. "And then we take down whoever wants to hurt my man."

Fuck, I love hearing her call me that.

I WATCH Hawk as he comes closer. My body's already reacting to him. He steps closer, his hand cupping my cheek, his thumb dragging over my lower lip. I open my mouth to protest time again, but he silences me with a kiss.

It's deep and consuming, his tongue invading my mouth, his teeth clashing against mine. It's a kiss that's like a fight, just like everything else with us. It's brutal and intense, and it leaves me dizzy and trembling.

He pulls away, his eyes locked onto mine, a wicked grin spreading across his face. He drops to his knees, his hands gripping my pants, yanking them down and off, exposing me to him completely. He lifts my legs, draping them over his shoulders, his face inches from my pussy.

I grip his head, my fingers tangling in his hair, my body tense with anticipation and nerves. He looks up at me, his eyes dark and intense.

"This is my pussy, Devin," he growls, his voice thick with lust. "Mine to touch. Mine to taste. Mine to fuck." He leans in, inhaling deeply, his eyes fluttering closed as he takes in my scent. I bite back a squeal.

"Hawk," I whisper, my voice trembling with need. "Please. I don't know how long I can wait."

He snaps his eyes open, his gaze sharp and intense. "If I want to eat this pussy, Devin, I fucking will," he growls, his voice leaving no room for argument. "And you're going to let me. And you'll sit there and be a good girl. Because you're mine. Every inch of you. Every part of you. Mine."

He's right. I am his. Completely and utterly. And as he leans in, his tongue licking a slow, deliberate line up my slit, I know I'm lost. To him. To this. To the pleasure only he can give me.

Hawk's tongue parts my folds, licking and exploring every inch of me with an expertise that leaves me gasping. He's slow and deliberate, his tongue circling my clit, applying just the right amount of pressure to make my hips buck against him. I grip his hair tighter, my body trembling as he devours me, his mouth and tongue working in a rhythm that has me seeing stars.

"Fuck, you taste good," he growls, his voice vibrating against my sensitive flesh, sending shivers down my spine. "I could eat you all day."

He slides a finger inside me, his tongue still lapping at my clit, his eyes locked onto mine. I moan, my body clenching around his finger, my breath coming in short gasps. He smirks, his finger moving in and out of me, his tongue keeping a steady rhythm against my clit.

"You're so tight, Devin," he murmurs, his voice thick with lust. "So wet. So fucking perfect. I can't wait to feel your pussy come all over my face."

He slides another finger inside me, his tongue flicking against my clit faster now, his fingers curling inside me, hitting that spot that makes my body sing. My orgasm builds, my body tenses, my breath hitches. He senses it too, his fingers moving faster, his tongue lapping at me with a fervor that has me crying out.

"That's it, sweetheart," he growls, his voice thick with need. "Come for me. Let me taste that sweet cum. Let me feel that pussy come all over my face."

His words push me over the edge, and I come with a cry, my body convulsing, my pussy clenching around his fingers, my cum gushing out of me, coating his face. He groans, his tongue slurping at me, his fingers still moving inside me, drawing out every last drop of my orgasm.

"Fuck, that's good," he murmurs, his voice thick with satisfaction. "Fucking soaking my face. You're such a good girl."

He continues to lick and finger me, his movements slowing, his touch gentle now, drawing out every last shiver of pleasure. I'm a trembling mess, my body limp, my breath coming in ragged gasps. He pulls his fingers out of me, his tongue giving one last lick to my clit before he looks up at me, his face glistening with my cum.

"Look at you, all flushed and satisfied," he murmurs, his voice soft but firm. "That's how you should always look, Devin. Like you've just been thoroughly fucked, claimed, and owned. By me."

He stands, his hands gripping my hips, pulling me up with him. He kisses me, his lips and tongue coated in my essence, the taste of me mixed with the taste of him. It's dirty and wrong, but it turns me on even more.

Fuck, what is wrong with me? I shouldn't want more of him, but I've known for a long time that I can't get enough of Hawk.

I don't know if I ever will.

TWENTY

My fingers dance across the keyboard, weaving through firewalls and encrypted data like a ghost in the machine. Beside me, Hawk leans in, his breath hot on my neck. His proximity sends shivers down me, a delicious mix of desire and danger I've become addicted to.

"Anything?" he asks, his voice low and tense. The barely contained violence in his tone makes my heart race.

I shake my head, frustration building. "Not yet. Your father's financials are clean – well, as clean as an addict's can be. But your uncle…" I trail off, my eyes narrowing as a new window pops up on my screen.

"What is it?" Hawk's hand tightens on my shoulder,

his grip possessive and bruising. I revel in the pain knowing it'll leave marks. His marks.

A slow, predatory smile spreads across my face. "Got him. Your uncle's phone just pinged at The Black Swan."

Hawk's eyebrows shoot up. "The bar Kazanov and Regina frequented?"

I nod, excitement coursing through me. "It's him, Hawk. Your uncle's the one behind this. And..." I pause, digging deeper into the data, breaking through layers of security that would take most hackers days to crack. "He's looking to hire more people. To kill you."

Hawk's eyes darken dangerously, a cold fury settling over his features. The look sends a thrill through me – I love seeing him like this, raw and lethal. "Then we need to move fast," he growls.

My fingers are already dancing across the keyboard again. "I'm on it. Setting up a meeting now, posing as the hitmen he's looking for." I create an entire digital footprint for our fake assassins in minutes, complete with dark web reviews and a history of successful hits.

As I work, I feel Hawk's gaze on me, intense and hungry. "You're incredible," he murmurs, leaning in to bite my neck, hard enough to leave bruises and teeth marks. I gasp, pleasure and pain intertwining.

"Save it for after we take down your uncle," I tease even as I lean into his touch craving more.

Within minutes, the trap is set. Hawk makes a few calls, assembling his team with ruthless efficiency. As we prepare to leave, he pulls me into his arms, his grip almost painfully tight.

"Stay close to me," he growls, his eyes boring into mine with an intensity that would frighten most people. To me, it feels like coming home. "I can't lose you. You're mine, Devin. The only thing in this world that matters."

I meet his gaze unflinchingly, matching his possessiveness with my own. "And you're mine, Hawk. Until the end."

He nods, then kisses me fiercely, all teeth and tongue and barely restrained violence. It leaves me breathless and wanting more.

The drive to the meeting site is tense, the air thick with anticipation. Hawk is disguised, nearly unrecognizable, but I can still see the coiled energy in his posture, the predator ready to strike. It's intoxicating.

As we pull up to the abandoned Rivers property, I scan the area, my mind processing a thousand details at once. "Your people are in position," I murmur, noting the subtle signs of surveillance. "I've looped the security cameras and set up a signal jammer. We're ghosts here."

Hawk nods, his eyes never leaving the entrance. "He must be desperate," he says, his voice cold. "Coming out in the open like this."

"He lost both Regina and Kazanov," I remind him, a hint of pride in my voice. We did that, together. "We've backed him into a corner. And cornered animals are the most dangerous."

We exit the car, Hawk's hand finding the small of my back as we approach the building. The touch grounds me, focuses my racing thoughts. In moments like these, I'm hyperaware of how perfectly we fit together – two broken, dangerous pieces forming a deadly whole.

Inside, the air is stale, dust motes dancing in the weak sunlight filtering through grimy windows. And there, in the center of the room, stands Hawk's uncle.

He looks older than when I saw him at the gala, lines of stress etched deep into his face. His eyes dart nervously between us as we approach.

"You're the ones who can... handle my problem?" he asks, his voice wavering slightly.

Hawk nods, his voice disguised. "For the right price. You mentioned specifics?"

The uncle's posture relaxes slightly. "Yes, yes. It needs to look like an accident. My nephew, Hawk

Rivers – he can't suspect foul play. Perhaps a car crash or..."

He doesn't get to finish. In one fluid motion, Hawk strips off his disguise, revealing himself. The uncle's face drains of color.

"H-Hawk?" he stammers. "What is this?"

"This," Hawk snarls, advancing on him, "is what happens when you try to take what's mine."

The first punch lands with a sickening crunch, and I watch with dark satisfaction as Hawk unleashes his fury. His movements are precise, calculated, each blow designed to inflict maximum pain without knocking his uncle unconscious. It's a cold, methodical brutality.

"Did you really think you could take what's mine?" Hawk growls, his voice terrifyingly calm as he continues his assault. "Did you think I wouldn't find out? That I wouldn't destroy everything you love in return?"

Movement in my peripheral vision catches my attention. My heart races as I process the new threat, my mind working overtime to analyze and react.

A figure emerges from the shadows, and my blood runs cold as I recognize Hawk's cousin, Thomas. The glint of metal in his hand has me moving before I can think.

"Hawk!" I scream as two shots ring out.

Time seems to slow. I see the surprise on Thomas's

face as I throw myself in front of Hawk. I don't feel the impact at first. There's just a sense of wrongness, of heat spreading across my abdomen. I hear more gunshots, see Thomas and Hawk's uncle crumple to the ground.

And then Hawk is there, his face a mask of shock and rage unlike anything I've ever seen. "Devin? Devin, no, no, no..."

I try to speak, to tell him I'm okay, but my mouth won't cooperate. Darkness creeps in at the edges of my vision. The last thing I'm aware of is Hawk's arms around me, his voice calling my name as consciousness slips away.

I don't care if I die, I think hazily. As long as he lives. As long as Hawk is safe. He's mine, and I protect what's mine – even if it costs me everything.

Then, nothing.

The world fades to black, and for a moment, I feel myself floating in a void. But then, like a computer rebooting, my senses slowly come back online. I hear frantic voices, feel the pressure of hands on my wound. My eyes flutter open, and I see Hawk's face, twisted with a mix of fury and fear I've never seen.

"Don't you dare leave me," he growls, his voice thick with emotion. "Do you hear me, Devin? You're mine, and I order you to stay at my side. I'll follow you into hell if I have to."

I want to respond, to reassure him, to tell him that I'd burn the world down to stay with him. But the darkness is pulling me under again. As I slip back into unconsciousness, one thought echoes in my mind: I've never seen Hawk lose control like this. And it's all because of me.

TWENTY-ONE

SIX YEARS AGO

The Day After Devin's 18th Birthday

I sit across from Devin's parents in their immaculate living room, my posture relaxed but my mind razor-sharp. Every detail of this conversation could impact my future with Devin, and I refuse to leave anything to chance.

"Mr. and Mrs. West," I begin, my voice steady and confident, "I've come to discuss my intentions toward your daughter. I want to marry Devin."

Mrs. West's eyes widen slightly while Mr. West's gaze intensifies. "That's... quite a statement, Mr. Rivers," he says. "Devin is only eighteen."

I nod, acknowledging his concern. "I'm aware of the age difference. But I also know that Devin is exceptional in every way. She's not a typical eighteen-year-old."

Mrs. West smiles softly. "No, she certainly isn't. But, Hawk, we've always planned for Devin to study overseas. To expand her skills and experiences. We don't want anything to hold her back."

I feel a wave of possessiveness at the thought of Devin leaving, but I keep my expression neutral. "I understand completely. I have no intention of hindering Devin's growth or ambitions. In fact, I want to support them."

Mr. West raises an eyebrow. "How so?"

I lean forward, my gaze steady. "I'm willing to wait until Devin feels ready to be my wife. But I won't let her leave for college until we're legally married. It's non-negotiable."

I see a flash of surprise in their eyes, but I press on before they can object. "While she's overseas, she'll have my protection. I'll ensure she's always guarded, though discreetly. I'm also arranging for her to learn various forms of self-defense. She'll be a master of the martial arts."

Mrs. West nods slowly, considering my words. "That's... thoughtful. I know she's always been an easy target for other girls her age. Even in our family."

A small smile tugs at my lips. "I'm aware. That's why I've asked Olivia to work with her on being more self-assured and assertive. Olivia has a way of bringing out Devin's confidence."

Mr. West chuckles. "That she does. You've certainly given this a lot of thought, Hawk."

"Devin is worth every moment of consideration," I reply, my voice low and intense. "I want to give her the world, but I also want to ensure she's safe and prepared for whatever challenges she might face."

The Wests exchange a look, having one of those silent conversations that long-married couples seem to excel at. Finally, Mr. West turns back to me.

"We appreciate your thoroughness, Hawk. And your willingness to support Devin's dreams." He pauses, then nods. "You have our approval."

Relief washes over me, though I don't let it show on my face. Instead, I stand, extending my hand to Mr. West. "Thank you. I promise to always put Devin's well-being first."

As we shake hands, Mrs. West adds, "Devin's in her room if you'd like to speak with her now."

I nod, thanking them both before making my way upstairs. I've never been in Devin's room, and I find myself curious about this private space of hers.

The door is slightly ajar, and I push it open without

knocking. The sight that greets me is far from a typical teenage girl's room. Instead of posters and frilly decorations, I'm met with a tech lair that would put most corporate IT departments to shame. Multiple monitors line the walls, cables snake across the floor, and the soft hum of powerful computers fills the air.

In the center of it all sits Devin, her fingers flying across a keyboard, her face illuminated by the glow of the screens. She's so engrossed in her work that she doesn't notice me at first.

I clear my throat, and she whirls around, her eyes wide with surprise. "Hawk? What are you doing here?"

I step into the room, closing the door behind me. My eyes never leave hers as I approach. "I came to see you, of course."

Devin's brow furrows. "But... how? My parents never let anyone up here, especially not..." She trails off, a blush creeping up her cheeks.

"Especially not men?" I finish for her, a smirk playing on my lips. "Let's just say I had an important conversation with your parents."

Her eyes narrow suspiciously. "What kind of conversation?"

I reach her chair, towering over her seated form. Slowly, deliberately, I place my hands on the armrests, caging her in. "The kind where I asked for their blessing to marry you."

Devin's breath catches, her eyes widening in shock. "You... what?"

TWENTY-TWO

My heart pounds in my chest as I stare up at Hawk, his words echoing in my ears. Marriage. He wants to marry me. The idea is both thrilling and terrifying, sending shockwaves through my system.

"I... I don't know what to say," I stammer, speech deserting me. "This is so unexpected."

Hawk's eyes bore into mine, intense and unyielding. "Say yes," he growls, his voice low and demanding. "Be mine, Devin. Completely."

A shiver runs down my spine at his tone, desire pooling in my belly. God, I want this. I want him. But...

"I want to go to college," I blurt out. "I need to be better, stronger. Not some weakling who can't stand by your side."

A dark smile spreads across Hawk's face. "I'll make sure you become everything you want to be," he promises. "As long as you marry me. I'll give you the world, Devin. All you have to do is say yes."

His words are intoxicating, a siren song of power and possibility. But a part of me rebels against the idea of being so thoroughly possessed even as another part craves it desperately.

"I... I don't want to be a nuisance in your life," I admit, hating how vulnerable I sound. "You have your empire to run, and I'll be away at school..."

Hawk's hand cups my face, his touch both gentle and possessive. "You could never be a nuisance," he says fiercely. "You're everything to me, Devin. Everything."

I lean into his touch, savoring the warmth of his skin against mine. But a thought nags at me, refusing to be silenced.

"If I agree," I say slowly, "you have to promise me something."

Hawk's eyes narrow. "What?"

I take a deep breath, steeling myself. "Promise you'll continue your life without me while I'm gone. If we're truly meant to be, when I'm done with school and learning to take better care of myself, I'll come back. If you still want me then, I'll be yours. Completely."

Anger flashes in Hawk's eyes. "I already know I want you," he growls. "I'll always want you."

For the first time in my life, I feel a surge of defiance. "Then prove it," I challenge. "Let me go, let me become who I need to be. And if our love is as strong as you say, it'll survive the separation. I don't want you calling me and texting me and trying to control me from a distance. You have to truly let me go. I want to learn and grow and become my own person."

Hawk's jaw clenches, his whole body radiating tension. "You're mine," he says, his voice dangerously low. "I don't share what's mine."

"I'm not asking you to share," I retort, surprised by my own boldness. "I'm asking you to wait. To let me prove that I'm worthy of standing by your side. That I can be the woman you need."

We glare at each other, the air between us crackling with tension. I see the struggle in Hawk's eyes, the war between his possessiveness and his desire to give me what I want.

"There's one more thing," I add, my voice barely above a whisper. "If I agree, we keep it a secret. Nobody but us and my parents can know until I'm ready to reveal it."

Hawk's eyes flash dangerously. "You want to hide our marriage?"

I nod, holding my ground despite the fear coursing through me. "I need to do this on my own terms, Hawk. I won't be seen as just your wife. I want to make my own name, my own reputation."

For a long moment, Hawk is silent, his gaze boring into mine. I can almost see the gears turning in his head, weighing the pros and cons of my conditions.

Finally, he speaks. "You drive a hard bargain, my little genius," he says, a hint of admiration in his voice. "But I have a condition of my own."

I raise an eyebrow, waiting.

"You'll wear my ring," he says. "It's non-negotiable."

I consider his request, my heart racing. "Agreed," I say finally.

He pulls a box out of his pocket and inside is a beautiful emerald ring, flanked by diamonds. He slips the ring on my finger and then meets my gaze. "You don't take this off. Ever."

"I won't. As long as you promise to live your life, not just wait for me."

Hawk grips my chin, and for a moment, I think he might refuse. But then he nods, a predatory smile spreading across his face.

"Very well, my love," he purrs. "We'll play this game your way. For now."

Before I can respond, he crushes his lips to mine in a

bruising kiss. I melt into him, all my doubts and fears evaporating in the heat of his passion.

As we break apart, both breathing heavily, I see a mix of triumph and hunger in Hawk's eyes. "You're mine now, Devin," he growls. "Never forget that."

I nod, a thrill of excitement and fear running through me. "And you're mine," I whisper back.

In this moment, I know I've made a deal with the devil. But as I look into Hawk's eyes dark with desire and possessiveness, I can't bring myself to regret it.

TWENTY-THREE

PRESENT

The gunshots still echo in my ears as I watch Devin crumple to the ground, her blood staining the concrete. Time seems to slow, my world narrowing to the sight of her pale face, her eyes fluttering closed.

"No, no, no," I mutter, dropping to my knees beside her. My hands press against her wound, warm blood seeping between my fingers. "Devin, stay with me. Don't you dare leave me."

The bodies of my uncle and cousin lie nearby, their unseeing eyes a testament to my rage. But I can't focus on them now. All that matters is the woman in my arms, her life slipping away with each passing second.

"Daniel!" I roar, my voice raw with panic. "Get the car. Now!"

I scoop Devin into my arms, cradling her against my chest as I rush toward the waiting vehicle. Her blood soaks into my shirt, a visceral reminder of how close I am to losing her.

"Drive," I bark as soon as we're inside. Daniel doesn't hesitate, peeling away from the scene with tires screeching.

I keep pressure on Devin's wound, my eyes never leaving her face. "Stay with me, love," I murmur, my voice cracking. "You're not allowed to die. You're mine, remember? Mine."

The drive to the hospital is a whirl of fear and desperate prayers to a God I've never believed in. When we slide to a halt at the emergency entrance, I'm out of the car before it fully stops, Devin limp in my arms.

"I need help!" I shout, bursting through the doors. "Gunshot wound. She's losing blood fast."

A flurry of activity erupts around us. Doctors and nurses swarm, taking Devin from my arms and rushing her away on a gurney. I try to follow, but a firm hand on my chest stops me.

"Sir, you need to let them work," a doctor says, her voice calm but firm. "We'll update you as soon as we can."

"Please," I beg, something I've never done in my life. "Save my wife."

She gives me a sad look. "We'll do our best." And leaves me behind.

I want to argue, to force my way through, but I know it would only waste precious time. Instead, I stiffly watch as they wheel Devin away.

The waiting room is a special kind of hell. I pace relentlessly, my clothes still stained with Devin's blood. Time loses all meaning as I wait for news, any news.

Olivia arrives first, her face pale with worry. "Hawk," she says, rushing to me. "What happened? Is she-"

"Surgery," I cut her off, unable to bear the thought of the alternative. "No word yet."

She nods, sinking into a nearby chair. We wait in tense silence, both lost in our own fears.

It's not long before Max appears, looking decidedly out of place in his rumpled clothes and thick-rimmed glasses. His presence surprises me – I knew he was more than just Devin's assistant, but I hadn't realized how close they were.

"Any news?" he asks, his voice tight with concern.

I shake my head, frustration bubbling up inside me. "Nothing yet."

The minutes crawl by like hours. Finally, a doctor approaches, his face grave. "Mr. Rivers?"

I'm on my feet in an instant. "How is she?"

"Ms. West is still in surgery," he says. "But we've run into a complication. She's lost a lot of blood, and with her rare blood type – RH negative – we're not sure we have enough in our bank."

My heart clenches. "I'm RH negative," I say immediately. "Take mine. Take as much as you need."

The doctor nods, relief evident on his face. "That could make all the difference. Follow me, please."

I turn to Olivia and Max. "Stay here. Let me know the moment there's any news."

They nod, and I follow the doctor, ready to give every drop of blood in my body if it means saving Devin.

The blood donation process seems to take an eternity, but finally, I'm back in the waiting room. Olivia and Max fill the silence with quiet conversation, but I can't focus on their words. My entire being is centered on Devin, willing her to survive.

After what feels like days, the surgeon appears, looking tired but satisfied. "Mr. Rivers?"

I stand, my heart in my throat. "Yes? How is she?"

The surgeon smiles slightly. "Ms. West is out of surgery. We were able to remove the bullet and repair the damage. Thanks to your blood donation, we were able to stabilize her."

Relief floods me, so intense it nearly brings me to my knees. "Thank God," I breathe.

"There is one more thing," the surgeon adds, his tone careful. "We were very fortunate that the bullet didn't hit any vital organs... or cause a miscarriage."

For a moment, I'm sure I've misheard. "Miscarriage?" I repeat, my voice low. My heartbeat slows to a crawl.

The surgeon nods. "Ms. West is approximately eight weeks pregnant. The fetus appears unharmed, but we'll be monitoring closely."

The world seems to tilt on its axis. Pregnant. Devin is pregnant. With my child. After all these years of separation, of waiting, we're going to have a family.

"Can I see her?" I ask, my voice rough with emotion.

The surgeon nods. "She's in recovery now. I'll have a nurse take you to her."

As I follow the nurse down the sterile hallway, my mind races. A baby. Our baby. Life finally feels right.

TWENTY-FOUR

Warm lips trail along my neck, pulling me from the depths of sleep. I groan, burying my face deeper into the pillow. "Hawk, let me sleep," I mumble, my voice thick with exhaustion.

His chuckle reverberates against my skin, dark and possessive. "Time to wake up, love. You need to eat to feed our baby."

I crack one eye open, meeting his intense gaze. "You're a dictator, you know that?" I grumble, but there's no real heat in my words.

His smile is predatory, yet tinged with genuine affection. "Perhaps. But I'm *your* dictator." His hand slides possessively over my still-flat stomach. "And our child's."

I can't help but lean into his touch, even as I roll my eyes. "Fine, fine. What's for breakfast, then?"

Instead of answering, Hawk scoops me up in his arms, cradling me against his chest. I yelp in surprise, my arms automatically winding around his neck.

"Hawk! I can walk, you know. I've been home from the hospital for over a week now. I feel fine."

He tightens his grip, his eyes darkening dangerously. "I'm not taking any chances. You need to rest."

I want to argue, but the memory of the terror in his eyes when I was shot silences me. This is the man who waited six years for me, who gave his blood to save my life. If carrying me to breakfast makes him feel in control, I can indulge him. For now.

He sets me in a chair at the dining table, his hands lingering possessively on my shoulders. The spread before us is impressive – all my favorites, I notice. Hawk has clearly gone out of his way to ensure I have everything I might want or need.

I finally ask what I've been wanting to for a while. "Why did you get the same tattoo I have?"

He cups my cheek and grins. "Because we're the same. Two halves of a whole."

That we are.

As we eat, Hawk fills me in on the latest family news. "My father's finally agreed to get help," he says, a hint of vulnerability breaking through his usual mask of control. "Real help this time, not just a quick rehab stint."

I reach out, squeezing his hand. "That's wonderful, Hawk. I hope it sticks this time."

He nods, his thumb tracing circles on my palm. "Me too. It's been... a long road." The pain in his voice is palpable, and I'm struck by how much he's allowing me to see.

I lean into him, offering silent support. His free hand comes to rest on my stomach again, a gesture that's become almost instinctive since we learned about the baby.

"I've been thinking," I say softly, watching his face. "Maybe it's time we tell people. About us being married, I mean."

Hawk's eyes flash with triumphant possession. "I've been ready to tell the world for six years," he growls, pulling me closer. "To let everyone know you're mine."

I laugh softly as a thrill runs through me at his intensity. "I know, I know. I just... I wanted to make my own name first. To prove I could stand beside you as an equal."

His grip on me tightens almost painfully. "You've always been my equal, Devin. My perfect match in every way. Even when you were that brilliant, infuriating eighteen-year-old who demanded I let her go."

I smile at the memory, tracing the line of his jaw. "You didn't make it easy."

"I told you I wouldn't wait idly," he reminds me, his voice low and dangerous. "You're mine, Devin. You always have been."

The possessiveness in his tone sends a pulse of heat through my body. "And you're mine," I whisper back, my nails digging into his skin slightly. "Don't forget that."

Hawk's eyes darken with desire and something deeper – a vulnerability he shows only to me. In one swift motion, he pulls me onto his lap, his mouth claiming mine in a bruising kiss that's equal parts possession and devotion.

When we finally break apart, both breathing heavily, I see the barely restrained hunger in his gaze. "Careful, Mrs. Rivers," he murmurs, his voice husky. "Or we might not make it out of this room for a while."

I laugh, the sound tinged with desire and genuine affection. "Is that a threat or a promise?"

"It's always a promise."

His answer is to stand, lifting me with him. As he carries me back to our bedroom, I can't help but marvel at the journey that brought us here. Our love may be intense, possessive, even toxic by some standards. But it's also deep, genuine, and unbreakable.

With Hawk's arms around me and our child growing inside me, I feel both owned and cherished, trapped and free. It's a paradox that defines us – two pieces forming a whole, bound by a love that defies all expectations.

The world isn't ready for what Hawk and I can do together.

The End

ABOUT THE AUTHOR

New York Times and USA Today Bestselling Author

Hi! I'm Milly Taiden. I love to write sexy stories featuring fun, sassy heroines with curves and growly alpha males with fur. My books are a great way to satisfy your craving for paranormal romance with action, humor, suspense and happily ever afters.

I live in Florida with my hubby, our son, and our fur babies: Stormy and Teddy. I have a serious addiction to all types of desserts.

I love to meet new readers, so come sign up for my newsletter and check out my Facebook page. We always have lots of fun stuff going on there.

SIGN UP FOR MILLY'S NEWSLETTER FOR LATEST NEWS!

http://eepurl.com/pt9q1

Find out more about Milly here:

www.millytaiden.com
milly@millytaiden.com

ALSO BY MILLY TAIDEN

Find out more about Milly Taiden here:

Email: millytaiden@gmail.com

Website: http://www.millytaiden.com

Facebook: http://www.facebook.com/millytaidenpage

Twitter: https://www.twitter.com/millytaiden

You can find a complete list of all my books by series and reading order at my website: millytaiden.com

Made in the USA
Columbia, SC
31 October 2024

fc4d39af-0dc0-4b62-86e6-d570a115e645R01